P9-CRH-166

Wedded Bliss

Penny Jordan   Carole Mortimer

Two brand-new stories in one volume,
especially written by your favorite authors to
celebrate Harlequin's 50th Anniversary!

There's nothing more exciting than a
wedding! Everyone basks in the happiness
the occasion brings, eager to see the bride
walk up the aisle and exchange vows with
the groom. Then the champagne starts to
flow and the party goes on into the night....

But the lead-up to the wedding is just as
much fun, and a lot can happen on the
way to the altar. Read on and share the
excitement as two couples make their very
different journeys that will take them up the
aisle to embark upon a life of wedded bliss!

PENNY JORDAN has been writing for more than fifteen years and has an outstanding record: over 100 novels published, including **Power Play**, which hit the *New York Times* bestseller list, and most recently, the phenomenally successful **To Love, Honor and Betray**. With over 60 million copies of her books in print worldwide and translations in more than seventeen languages, Penny Jordan has established herself as an internationally acclaimed author. She was born in Preston, in Lancashire, England, and she now lives with her husband in a beautiful fourteenth-century house in rural Cheshire.

CAROLE MORTIMER has a long-standing reputation as one of Harlequin®'s most popular authors. Readers love her likable heroines and strong, charismatic heroes, so it's not surprising that over 40 million copies of her books have been distributed internationally. She says, "I was born in England, the youngest of three children—I have two older brothers. I started writing in 1978, and have now written 100 books for Harlequin. I have four sons—Matthew, Joshua, Timothy and Peter— and a bearded collie dog called Merlyn. I'm in a very happy relationship with Peter senior. We're best friends as well as lovers, which is probably the best recipe for a successful relationship. We live on the Isle of Man."

PENNY JORDAN
CAROLE MORTIMER

Wedded Bliss

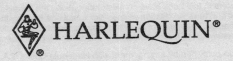

HARLEQUIN®

TORONTO • NEW YORK • LONDON
AMSTERDAM • PARIS • SYDNEY • HAMBURG
STOCKHOLM • ATHENS • TOKYO • MILAN • MADRID
PRAGUE • WARSAW • BUDAPEST • AUCKLAND

If you purchased this book without a cover you should be aware that this book is stolen property. It was reported as "unsold and destroyed" to the publisher, and neither the author nor the publisher has received any payment for this "stripped book."

ISBN 0-373-12031-1

WEDDED BLISS

First North American Publication 1999.

Copyright © 1999 by Harlequin Books S.A.

The publisher acknowledges the copyright holders of the individual works as follows:

THEY'RE WED AGAIN!
Copyright © 1999 by Penny Jordan

THE MAN SHE'LL MARRY
Copyright © 1999 by Carole Mortimer

All rights reserved. Except for use in any review, the reproduction or utilization of this work in whole or in part in any form by any electronic, mechanical or other means, now known or hereafter invented, including xerography, photocopying and recording, or in any information storage or retrieval system, is forbidden without the written permission of the publisher, Harlequin Enterprises Limited, 225 Duncan Mill Road, Don Mills, Ontario, Canada M3B 3K9.

All characters in this book have no existence outside the imagination of the author and have no relation whatsoever to anyone bearing the same name or names. They are not even distantly inspired by any individual known or unknown to the author, and all incidents are pure invention.

This edition published by arrangement with Harlequin Books S.A.

® and TM are trademarks of the publisher. Trademarks indicated with ® are registered in the United States Patent and Trademark Office, the Canadian Trade Marks Office and in other countries.

Printed in U.S.A.

Contents

They're Wed Again!
by
Penny Jordan

CHAPTER ONE

'AUNT BELLE! You look *wonderful*, positively glowing...'

'Shouldn't that be *my* line to *you*?' Isabelle smiled as she hugged her newly married niece, and then stepped back to admire her wedding dress.

'I'm sorry about the mix-up with the invitations,' Joy apologised. 'But Great-Aunt Alice insisted on helping Mum to write them, and you *know* what she's like.' She pulled a wry face. 'She completely forgot that you and Luscious Lucius got divorced simply ages ago, and sent you both joint invitations to his address...'

'"Luscious Lucius". You still call him that, do you?' Isabelle teased her niece, smiling a warm look at Joy's new husband.

'Oh, Andy doesn't mind,' Joy laughed back. 'After all, Luc *is* his cousin, and besides—' she gave her new husband a mock stern look '—Andy has always thought that *you* are gorgeously sexy—for an older woman...'

As the groom went pink, and tugged at his cravat, Isabelle raised her eyebrows. She was thirty-four, almost thirty-five, to Joy's twenty-three—not yet in her dotage, surely?

At Joy's age she and Luc had already been married for close on two years. They had married far too immature—a girl whom marriage had hot-housed into a woman. And while Luc might have loved the girl he had married, he had certainly ceased to love the woman that girl had become.

As she had told Luc at the time, she'd thought it grossly unfair that he had refused to acknowledge and appreciate the stresses that her career had placed on her, the anxiety that being the main breadwinner in their household had caused her. And then, on top of that anxiety, to have Luc complain that she was never at home, that she valued her job more than she did him, had been just too much for her to endure, and had ultimately caused the series of destructive rows which had eventually led to their divorce.

'Luc, I have hardly any time to myself,' she had pointed out to him during one of their arguments. 'When I *am* at home, I have housework to do, food to buy—this house doesn't clean itself, you know. I'm the one who has to worry about paying the mortgage and keeping the cupboards filled—all you have to worry about is your precious studying. Sometimes I think that is all you do think about—care about!'

Belle could still remember how his face had darkened, his eyes clouding as he'd turned away from her, his head seeming to hang a little. At over six foot he was much, much taller than her, but as he'd moved away from her then he'd looked oddly shrunken and defeated, humiliated and humbled somehow, and along with her anger she had felt a sense of anguish and pain, a sharp flash of panic which she'd quickly pushed to one side.

If she had thought about the subject at all before they had married, she had assumed naively that their marriage would be an idyll, a continuation of the hours, and days, and the very occasional stolen weekends they had managed to snatch since their first meeting earlier in the year when she, newly graduated and working for the high-powered city firm of financial analysts where she had been lucky to get a job, had been introduced by a friend to the brilliant young mathematician who had turned his back on the profitable world of commerce and finance and who, idealistically, had opted instead to devote himself to further study and ultimately a career as a university lecturer.

It had been a private joke between them in those early days that she was the one with the large salary and the company car, whilst he was the one still eking out a meagre living on a grant. But there had been no doubt in Belle's mind about her feelings, her love for Luc, and she had admired him intensely for his dedication and his idealism.

'I want to marry you...' Luc had told her longingly a few months into their courtship. 'I want us to be together for always. But I can barely afford to support myself, never mind a wife...'

'We could live on my salary,' Belle had told him sunnily, far too deeply in love with him to care how they financed their lives, just as long as they shared them.

If anyone had warned her then that her job, her earnings, which had made it possible for them to be together, would one day be the cause of them breaking up, she would have laughed in immediate denial.

Her love for Luc and his love for her had been so strong, so meant by fate, that she'd been sure nothing could ever make them part.

She might have been in the vanguard of a movement that had women taking on a much more prominent role in financing their own and their partner's lives, but striking a blow for equality had been the last thing on Belle's mind when, a few years into their marriage, she had persuaded Luc that it made more sense for them to buy a house now that they were married than for her to go on sharing his cramped rented accommodation. They could afford the mortgage after all. She had just been promoted and had received a good raise.

'You mean *you* can afford it,' Luc had corrected her gently, but Belle hadn't really heard him. She had been far too busy excitedly studying the house details she had brought home with her, dreaming already of how she would decorate their new home.

And in the end Luc had gone along with her wishes, and they had bought the pretty village property they had both fallen for in the small, and in those days undeveloped village within reasonably easy commuting distance of London and close to Cambridge, where Luc eventually hoped to get a university post.

'I won't be able to use my bike to get to college any more,' Luc had protested when they had first gone to see the house.

'You can travel by train, like I do,' Belle had pointed out. 'We can travel to the station together in my car.'

'What about the days when you leave at six and don't get back until nine or ten?' Luc had reminded her, but Belle had been so desperately in love with the house, so sure it was perfect for them, that eventually he had given way—as she had known he would.

They had celebrated their first night of owning the house in the big double bedroom in front of the fireplace, lying on their duvet on the bare floorboards.

Luc, always romantic, had insisted on lighting a fire in the hearth, and the room had smelled of woodsmoke and candles. There had been a problem getting the electricity turned on, Belle remembered, and she had gone to try to sort it out. In her absence Luc had been out and bought candles—hundreds of them, or so it had seemed. They had lit her way up the stairs where Luc had carefully and formally ushered her into their bedroom.

In their soft glow Luc's face had taken on a sternness, a maturity which had both startled her a little and thrilled her. She'd become so used to his gentle, easygoing acceptance of whatever plans she made, that to see him looking so purposeful and determined had touched a little feminine nerve inside her that had made her ache with longing for him.

'This house is our home,' Luc told her as he started to undress her. 'Our home, Belle. We'll work on it, shape it, share in it together... I know it's *your* salary that's made it possible for us to buy it, but it takes more than money to make a home, and I want our home to be something we've *both* worked for...'

There was a warning there for her to heed, but she neglected to do so, shivering a little in the cool evening air, despite the warmth of Luc's smoky fire, snuggling up close to him as he removed the last of their clothing, opening her mouth eagerly to the hungry passion of his as he started to kiss her.

The physical attraction between them had been immediate and intense right from the start; Luc, three, nearly four years her senior, had technically at least been the more experienced of the two of them, but, as he had freely and adoringly admitted to Belle, she had brought to their relationship and to him a sexual intensity and an emotional openness that made him feel that everything he had experienced before, everything he had thought he knew, had been merely a pale shadow of their shared reality.

Now, with their kisses growing deeper and deeper, and the warm, silk-rough glide of Luc's hands over her eager body, Belle forgot how cold it was, how cheerless the empty, unfurnished room; she forgot, too, the hassle she had had over their unconnected electricity supply, the irritation she had experienced with Luc because he had been so engrossed in his studies that he had forgotten to notify the authorities in time to have the supply reconnected before they moved in. What did that kind of electricity matter when the variety *they* created between them was so intense that it could fuel a whole universe?

The duvet was soft and inviting, even if at the back of Belle's mind lay the knowledge that it would have to be washed before it could go anywhere near the new bed she intended to persuade Luc to agree to her buying; the glow from the can-

dles was doing wonderful things to the soft curves
of her body and Luc's, and the glow in Luc's eyes
was making her burn so hotly for him that her trem-
ulous, almost panting breath was threatening to blow
those candles closest to them out.

'Luc…'

Wantonly she reached for him, pressing her open
mouth to each hollow and curve of his candlelight-
shadowed body, feeling him tense and shudder in
wild reaction to her sensuous caresses.

Her tongue-tip teased the dark arrowing of hair
that spread with delicious invitation down the length
of his torso, a rich, fertile valley all excitingly male,
yielding a harvest that Belle already knew full well
more than lived up to its promise. There was an
idealistic intensity about Luc that he brought to everything he did, but most especially to his love for
her.

She was his first real true love. He had once told
her in the early days of their relationship that she
would always be his one true love.

Belle loved him just as intensely, but there was a
practicality about her nature which made her sometimes feel just a little impatient of Luc's idealism
and his total lack of interest in anything material.

Of course, like him, she agreed that no amount of
money or material possessions could make up for a
lack of love; that what they had, what they *shared*,
was worth more than a king's ransom, a hundred
kings' ransoms, but… But just think how wonderful
it would have been tonight if they had been making
love in their new bed, the handsome king-sized one
she had seen in the small exclusive handmade fur-

niture shop just outside Cambridge, a bed with a wonderful hand-carved headboard. They could have their initials carved into it, and some special symbol to represent their love...

And then, as Luc's tenderly roving hands touched those most secret, sacred places of her body, she forgot all about the new bed and the mess the dusty floor would be making of their duvet, as a small moan of blissful pleasure escaped her lips.

She remembered about it the following day, though, as she complained to Luc about the dust-marks on the duvet and the candle wax that had fallen on it.

'It's a duvet—a piece of fabric. It will wash,' Luc had defended.

'Oh, yes, it will wash,' Belle agreed, tight-lipped. 'But not here and not by me. For one thing we don't possess a washing machine, and for another, even if we did, we don't have any electricity supply to run it.'

'Look, I'm sorry about that. I've already explained, Professor Lind wanted to ask my opinion about...'

Professor Lind was something of an idol to Luc, who desperately wanted to emulate the older man's academic achievements. Belle had met him several times but sensed that, like Luc, he was rather contemptuous of her much more materially based world. She also rather suspected that the professor felt Luc had made a mistake in marrying her, and when she had taxed Luc with this he had looked a little embarrassed and finally admitted that the professor *had* counselled him against getting married.

'He doesn't think any man should get married until he's over thirty,' he had told Belle ruefully, adding huskily, 'But then he's obviously never met a woman like you...never been in love...'

Discussing the duvet reminded Belle of the bed she had seen but, predictably, Luc objected the moment she had told him where she had seen it.

'It will be far too expensive for us,' he told her, his voice suddenly unusually curt and hard.

'Oh, Luc...I want us to have something special, passed on not from either of our parents, something that's ours...' she told him softly, moving towards him, intending to snuggle into his arms.

But to her chagrin he turned away from her, his face unexpectedly grim as he told her sharply, 'I thought we already had something special.'

'The house...' Belle agreed. 'Oh, yes, but I want it to be furnished as specially as it deserves, and—'

'No, Belle, *not* the house,' Luc told her distantly. 'I was referring to our love itself...'

They made up the quarrel on that occasion, but the issue of the new bed remained unresolved—until Belle thought she had found an ideal way of circumventing it.

Christmas was less than six weeks away, and the bed she coveted was tantalisingly on display in the small Cambridgeshire store where she had first viewed it.

One night, after they had made love and then were lying sensually entwined in the cramped space of the old three-quarter bed Luc's parents had given them, Belle tentatively raised the subject of a new bed again.

'I really loved that one I told you about,' she told Luc softly. 'And it would look wonderful here in this house...this room...'

Their house was old, eighteenth century and cottagey, and it cried out for sturdy, hand-made proper furniture, but of course such furniture was expensive.

'It would make a wonderful Christmas present to ourselves,' she wheedled softly in Luc's ear. He had proved increasingly stubborn of late about her contribution to their household, refusing to allow her to spend her unexpectedly high bonus on furniture, telling her that it was her money—not theirs.

'Don't you understand...? Can't you see...? I've seen the look on the faces of your friends, your family, when they come round here. They know there's no way *we* could afford to live somewhere like this, to buy a house like this, whilst *I'm* still virtually having to live on a grant...'

'You earn extra from the private tuition you give,' Belle protested.

Luc gave a harsh laugh.

'*Extra!* A pittance...*peanuts* compared to what you're earning. Look, I know what you're saying about the bed, and I do understand... But Belle, please, just this once, please indulge me. There's something... Trust me, Belle.'

'Well, if you insist,' Belle agreed, but secretly she was already planning to surprise him on Christmas Eve with the delivery of the new bed and the headboard. She would tell him that it was a present to both of them—which it was, of course. And he would understand. She knew he would.

When she went in to order the bed a week later, she soothed her conscience by telling herself that it was just silly male pride that was making Luc so difficult over it, and that he would soon forget all about his veto once he had seen how beautifully it suited the house.

At work the run-up to Christmas was hectic, a frenetic mixture of deadlines and glittery, no-expenses-spared client parties.

In Cambridge Luc's college was empty of students for the Christmas break, enabling Luc to take full advantage of the college library and its other facilities for his own studies. But in order to help out with the mortgage he had taken on more and more private tuition, leaving him less and less time for his own work.

'Pure maths at Luc's level requires a devotion and commitment which is almost on a par with that once required by the priesthood,' Luc's mentor told Belle severely when she gave in to Luc's quiet insistence and accompanied him to Professor Lind's pre-Christmas drinks party—a sedate affair, held in the chilly monastic starkness of his college rooms, the only food and drink on offer his housekeeper's home-made and deeply unpleasant mince pies and a sherry which made Belle grit her teeth.

'You know I only drink champagne,' she told Luc plaintively. After the luxury of vintage champagne and the delicious nibbles provided by her wealthy clients, Mrs Oakes' mince pies and the professor's sherry, like the high-minded academic conversation, were not to Belle's taste at all.

She *did* notice, though, how one of the professor's other students, a quiet, demure young woman with unexpectedly critically cool blue eyes, reacted in a way that was a good ten degrees *less* frosty when it was *Luc* who was addressing her and not Belle herself.

Not that Belle felt remotely threatened by or jealous of Harriet's obvious attraction to her husband. Why should she? Luc loved *her*, and would love her even more when they were cosily tucked up together in their lovely new bed with its wonderful headboard, she promised herself, and she happily contemplated writing a cheque to pay for it.

It had taken bribery and cajolery on a heroic scale to get her boss to agree that she could skip the firm's Christmas Eve get-together so that she could be at home with Luc when the bed was delivered. She had hardly seen anything of him over the previous month, or so it seemed, and she was looking forward to spending her few precious days off with him.

They were going to his parents for dinner on Christmas Day, and hers on Boxing Day, but they would have at least one night together in their new bed.

When she woke up on Christmas Eve morning Belle was so excited that she couldn't eat her breakfast. The house they had bought, their home, was everything that she wanted. It had the potential to make a wonderful home, and there was even the prospect of converting the loft above the garage into a self-contained bedsit, should the day arrive when they needed the services of a nanny.

Certainly, they both wanted children, but they had agreed that they were too young for them as yet. Luc wanted to wait until he had finished his studies, and from the tone of his conversation Belle had guessed that he would want her to give up her own job once they did have a family. She was not so sure that was something she would want to do, but there was plenty of time for her to talk Luc round to her point of view.

It was a pity that the bed had been so expensive, otherwise she might have been able to treat them to a visit to the January sales...

They desperately needed a decent sofa, and Belle rather liked the idea of them having two instead of the traditional one and a couple of armchairs. The cottage had a good-sized sitting room-cum-family room, as well as its large kitchen-cum-dining room, and on the other side of the entrance hall there was, much to her delight, a very respectably sized and pretty drawing room which ran the full length of the house. Plenty of scope for her home-making talents there. And the fact that the previous owners had been elderly meant that none of the attractive original features had been removed.

'You're looking very pleased with yourself,' Luc commented as he bent to kiss the top of her head and reach past her for the coffee pot.

'Mmm...' she agreed lazily, arching her neck and inviting him without a word to nuzzle the soft warm skin there.

'What have you got me for Christmas? I hope it's

something very special,' she teased him, knowing full well that the only thing she really wanted from him, the gift she valued above everything else, was the one she already had: the gift of his love for her, his commitment to her.

'Well, I might just…' he began, and then stopped theatrically, his eyes sparkling with love and happiness as he teased her back. 'No guessing, though. You're just going to have to wait until tomorrow.'

'Tomorrow.' Belle pouted. 'But I thought we'd… I'm going to give you *my* present *today*. Tomorrow we're going to your parents…'

'Not until lunchtime,' Luc reminded her.

'It's going to be a very busy time,' Belle sighed. 'First dinner with your family, and then we're going to my parents on Boxing Day.'

The two families, who had not known one another before Luc and Belle had met, had become firm friends, and they lived close enough to make visiting one another quite easy, often sharing their homes with each other's families at special times like Christmas. On Christmas Day night Belle's parents, her elder sister and her husband and their two young children were joining Luc's parents and other members of his family. As a country vicar, Luc's father lived in a vicarage more than large enough to house everyone overnight, even if his small stipend meant that he could never afford to comfortably heat the vast Victorian church property.

Belle liked Luc's family, even if she sometimes found them a trifle unworldly compared with the people she mixed with in her working life. Certainly their values and beliefs were very much in tune with those of her own parents, and she particularly liked Luc's uncle and his wife, and their thirteen-year-old son who shared so much of a family resemblance with Luc that Belle had not been surprised when Luc's mother had told her that Andy looked just the same as Luc had done at his age.

Luc's father had studied theology at Cambridge, and there was a tradition in the family of its male members being Cambridge men.

Because they were spending so much time away from home over Christmas, Luc and Belle had agreed that it would be a waste to have a real Christmas tree, and one of Belle's clients had presented her with an artistic and very expensive Christmas arrangement from one of London's top florists, made up of bare twigs and glass baubles, which had caused Luc to raise his eyebrows a little.

'Don't you like it?' Belle had asked him.

'It's...it's very artistic,' Luc had replied cautiously, and then had added a rueful admission, 'At home we always have a huge tree loaded with masses of stuff. Not very arty, I suppose, but it always seems...right. Vicars' wives always have to recycle everything, and Ma used to encourage me to make my own decorations when I was small... Not very aesthetic, I know, but for me the real spirit of Christmas is the thought behind the gift, not its material value.'

He was right, of course, and Belle knew it, shared his sentiments, but somehow he had made her feel that her values were glossy and worthless and even, in some belittling way, that *she* was glossy and worthless too.

Today, though, was Christmas Eve, and very soon their own special Christmas present was going to arrive. And every Christmas from now on, when they woke up in their special bed, when they made love in it, they would remember this, their first Christmas in their new home. Belle couldn't wait to see the bed with its special headboard in situ, to polish and admire it.

It was almost lunchtime when the van finally arrived in the narrow country lane outside their house.

'What's this?' Luc frowned as the driver got out. 'They must be looking for somewhere else. We haven't ordered anything...'

'Yes, we have,' Belle corrected him excitedly, craning her neck so that she could see out of the window as the men went to the rear of the van. 'Well, *I* have. It's our Christmas present...well, mine to you...to us...to the house. It's the bed, Luc, the one I told you about...with the wonderful headboard,' she hurried on.

'The one we agreed we wouldn't have because it was too expensive?' Luc asked her quietly.

But Belle was oblivious to the cold undertone to his voice, too busy watching what was going on outside the window to be aware of the hurt look in his eyes as she agreed flippantly, 'That's the one.'

'You went ahead and bought it without telling me, despite what we'd agreed...'

Now Belle did look at him, alerted to his feelings by the ominous tone of his voice.

'I thought you'd be pleased,' she told him. 'It's a present...a surprise. Luc...what is it? Where are you going?' she demanded frantically as he turned his back on her and started to walk towards the back door.

'Luc, come back,' she pleaded, but it was too late, and she couldn't run after him because the delivery men were already coming up the path with their new bed.

Luc would come round when he saw how wonderful their bedroom looked with the bed and its headboard proudly adorning it, Belle decided two hours later, when the men had gone and she was standing in the doorway of their bedroom admiring her new acquisition. They would need to get some different bedding now, she acknowledged, frowning a little as she studied the pretty floral set they had been given as a wedding present. Somehow it just didn't do the new bed justice.

Luc had sanded and polished the old floorboards shortly after they had moved in, and they certainly set the bed off perfectly. It was, she knew, the kind of bed that demanded heavy Irish linen sheets scented with lavender, old-fashioned bed linen, all the traditional touches.

Luc would love that, waking up smelling of lavender... Luc... where was he? He had been gone a long time. She hoped he'd...

It was almost half an hour later when another van pulled up outside the house, a much shabbier, older one than the one which had delivered their new bed and its accoutrements, and, to her astonishment, she saw Luc climbing out of the driver's door.

'Luc.' She went to the front door and opened it,

calling out anxiously to him. 'Where have you been?'

'To get your Christmas present,' he told her grimly.

Her Christmas present. In that old van… What on earth…? Warily she walked to the front gate and opened it, staring into the back of the van as Luc unlocked and raised the shutter door.

'What is it? What have you got in there?' she asked him uncertainly.

'I've already told you. Your Christmas present.'

As the last of the fading daylight filled the van and she saw inside it Belle's heart gave a shocked bound. There, in pieces, inside the van, was an old-fashioned bedframe, an obviously newly bought mattress and, tucked along one side of it, covered in a piece of old sheeting was the unmistakable shape of a wooden headboard.

'Luc…what have you done—' she began, and then stopped as he turned round and she saw his face.

She had never seen him look so bleak…so distant…so alien from her and to her.

'Very much the same as you've done. I've bought us a Christmas present. A new bed. For us…for you…' he told her in a voice that was icily polite and icily distant.

'That isn't new…the frame's old…' Belle began defensively. 'It looks…'

'It looks what?' Luc challenged her. 'It looks as though your colleagues…and your clients…would laugh at it, turn their materialistic designer noses up at it. Well, for your information, this bed belonged to my grandparents. They slept in it...cherished it...cared for it and valued it, just as my parents have done.'

'It's... It's...' Belle just didn't know what to say, and then, as Luc climbed into the van, the sheeting slipped off the headboard and the colour left her face completely. Unlike the frame itself, the headboard was quite plainly new. She could tell that because of the pretty carving on it, entwining their initials and the date of their marriage.

'Luc... You bought...' she began, but Luc was already shaking his head.

'I bought *nothing* apart from the mattress,' he told her grimly. 'The wood, good solid English oak, belonged to the father of one of my pupils. He gave it to me in exchange for his son's tuition. I did the carving myself. It isn't as fancy nor, I dare say, as desirable as the one you've bought, but...'

'You carved it...' Belle stopped him. '*You* carved it...'

'Yes.' Luc told her curtly, pushing the cloth back over it. 'But of course I realise that it won't come anywhere near to matching the one you've *bought*. The one *I* couldn't afford to buy you. It doesn't matter what I do or what I say, what I give you...how much I love you. The fact remains that you're the one who's supporting us both, financing us both...'

'Luc, what does *that* matter?' Belle protested. 'And besides, that's only temporary. When you get your fellowship...

'Oh, Luc, I love you so very much, and I love the headboard as well,' Belle told him tenderly—and she meant it.

* * *

Luc's gift to her, his bed, was installed in their bedroom whilst the one she had bought was relegated to one of the guest bedrooms. They made up their quarrel, and the ones that followed it, but with each one the fabric of their marriage grew a little thinner, until eventually the day came when neither of them could be bothered to repair the worn patches any longer.

The crux came one weekend, when Belle arrived home early from an overseas conference to find that Luc, who had attended a dinner party in Cambridge the night before, had stayed over in Harriet Parish's rooms.

Luc protested in vain that it was all completely innocent, that he had simply had too much to drink to want to risk driving, that he loved her and that Harriet was simply a fellow student...a friend...

In the row that followed they said so many ugly and hurtful things to one another that Belle knew there was no going back. Not this time...

'You're so damn materialistic, you wouldn't know real value if it hit you on the head,' Luc accused her at one point during their argument. 'Money, money—that's all that matters to you.'

'Perhaps it would matter more to you if you were the one who earned it,' Belle retaliated. 'It's all very well for you, sitting up there above the rest of us in your ivory tower, Luc, but you seem to forget that without my earnings there would be no ivory tower for you to live in...'

And so it went on, the pair of them tearing at the precious fabric of their vulnerable marriage, rending it, ripping it, destroying it, in a frenzy of bitterness and petty resentments.

Belle moved out of the house that weekend and she never moved back.

Six weeks later she filed for divorce, refusing to even discuss with Luc any possibility of them getting back together. Ironically, the only thing she took from their marital home was the bed and headboard—not the one she had bought, that she had left behind, and for all she knew it was still there in the house with Luc, who had bought out her share of their marital home.

No, the headboard, the one that still graced the head of the bed in her small London home, was the one that Luc had made for her. Not that she had intended that to happen. The men she had sent to collect the other headboard and bed from the spare room had made a mistake, and somehow or other she had never bothered to correct it.

CHAPTER TWO

'I MUST admit that Mum was stunned when you said that Luc had come round to deliver the invitation to you himself,' Joy, the happy bride, was saying now. 'I mean, we realised soon enough about the mistake. What on earth did he say? You must have been so surprised to open the door to see him there...'

'Mmm...'

'Luc, I was just saying to Belle that she must have been really surprised to open her front door and find you there,' Joy repeated breezily as her new husband's cousin suddenly materialised at Belle's side, apparently oblivious to the interest the fact that the two of them were standing amicably together was causing amongst their fellow wedding guests.

Luc's dark river-green eyes met Belle's honey-gold ones, exchanging a silent message.

'What on earth did you say to her? I mean, you hadn't spoken to one another for years...'

'Joy...' Andy cautioned his new bride, explaining to Belle and Luc, 'I think it must be the champagne on top of an empty stomach. She told me when we walked back down the aisle that she'd had three glasses whilst she was getting ready this morning...'

'No, four...' Joy corrected him, and then giggled.

'Darling, the photographer wants you,' her mother

announced, coming up to the newly married pair and
urging them to follow her.

'Oh, no more photographs,' Joy was complaining
as her mother led her away.

'Saved by the flashbulb,' Luc commented humor-
ously to Belle after they had gone.

'Mmm… You could hardly have told her what
really happened, could you?'

'What? That you took one look at me, went white
and practically fainted into my arms,' Luc commented.

'I'd been in bed with flu. I hadn't eaten anything
for three days…' Belle defended herself. 'Besides,'
she added slyly, 'I don't think *you'd* have wanted
me telling Andy that you carried me upstairs to bed
and started to undress me…'

'I did no such thing…'

'Yes, you did. My robe—'

'Your robe came off when I trod on the belt you
had left undone as I picked you up. And I had to
take you upstairs. All you have downstairs is your
garage and an entry hall… And besides, if you will
go completely naked under your robe… It was a
freezing cold February day. I just wanted to get you
somewhere warm. You frightened me to death, passing out like that. Mind you, I wasn't surprised. You
were far too thin and frail…'

'I told you, I'd been ill. Which is why—'

'Goodness me, you two look very cosy. How long
have you been married now? It must be over ten
years, and still no children! Well, they say, don't
they, that if you've none to make you laugh then
you've none to make you cry?'

Great-Aunt Alice...

Belle gave Luc a speaking look above the elderly lady's head. There was no point in trying to explain her error, especially not when....

'Aunt Alice...there you are...' Carol, Belle's sister and the mother of the bride, came hurrying back, looking harassed as she put her arm around their elderly relative.

'Darling, I'm so sorry about all of this. You'll never guess what she's done now,' she hissed in a whisper to Belle, but before she could elucidate, David, her husband, was hurrying up to her telling her that the caterers wanted to speak urgently to her.

'Shame,' Luc commented, giving Belle a small smile as he watched his ex-sister-in-law's departing back. 'Now we'll never know just what it is that Great-Aunt Alice has done...'

'You mean what *else* she's done,' Belle corrected him drolly, returning his smile with a look in her eyes that caused a passing waitress, who was not aware of their divorced status, to reflect rather ruefully on the enviable ability of some couples to keep a passionate intensity in their relationship which was now only an increasingly blurred memory in her own. Mind you, she had to acknowledge fairly, it would be a very odd woman indeed who did *not* feel a twinge of sensual female excitement at the sight of a man as attractive as Luc. Her own husband, kind man though he was, was not exactly charismatic.

'Mmm... I must say I was rather taken aback when I received the wedding invitation addressed to both of us.'

'It *was* very thoughtful of you to take the trouble to deliver it by hand,' Belle responded mock demurely, her honey-gold eyes dancing with laughter—and something else, something deeper and warmer that made Luc's breath catch slightly in his throat. Belle had always had that special something about her, a warmth and energy, a vibrancy. He had noticed it about her the very first time they had met.

'I was in London anyway,' Luc reminded her, attempting to make light of the incident, but, like hers, his eyes glowed hot with remembered emotion, giving him away.

'It's rather warm in here. What do you say to us taking the opportunity to get a little fresh air before we go in for the wedding breakfast?' Luc suggested.

'People will talk,' Belle pointed out to him. 'They'll wonder what's going on...'

'Mmm...' Luc agreed, placing his hand on the back of her waist and gently guiding her towards the exit to the hotel's gardens.

'I'm glad to see that you've put some weight back on.'

'I'd been ill,' Belle reminded him.

'You were skin and bone,' Luc continued. 'I thought...'

'That I'd been pining away for you over the years?'

Luc gave her a direct look.

'No. I didn't think that, Belle. I've got my faults, I know that, but suffering from delusions has never been one of them.'

'Who says it would have been a delusion?' Belle surprised them both by admitting a little gruffly.

'There was a time when we first parted...' She paused, and then, her face clouding, told him, 'Oh, Luc...I was so dreadfully unhappy then, and—'

She stopped abruptly. It wasn't like her to admit to any kind of vulnerability, and she could see that Luc was as surprised by her admission as she herself was.

'If we weren't here...' he began, and Belle shook her head chidingly. But that didn't stop a tiny thrill of excitement running dangerously down her spine.

It *had* been a shock to open her front door that day and discover that her unwanted visitor was no less than Luc, her ex-husband, to whom she had neither spoken nor seen since their divorce seven years before.

The sight of him standing there, so tall and darkly handsome, so excessively and alluringly male and mature, had been more than her already overloaded weakened defence system had needed to send it into complete chaos.

As she'd clung to the front door she'd been able to literally feel the blood draining down through her body at the same time as a weakening rush of dizzying faintness poured swiftly through it.

She had known what was going to happen, *known* she was going to faint, but at the same time she had known too that she simply did not have the strength or the will-power to halt it. Her last thought as Luc had masterfully reached out to catch her up in his arms had been how good he smelled, how good he *felt*...how good it was to be held so protectively and so safely in his arms.

Her faint had only lasted a couple of minutes, but

that had been long enough for Luc to close her front door and carry her upstairs, through the living room of her small mews house and into her bedroom.

She had come round to discover that she was lying on her bed completely naked, with Luc leaning anxiously over her calling her name.

Even now, more than three months later, she still couldn't quite account for the effect, the erotic charge, the sheer inconsistency of the emotions which had allowed her to experience a previously unknown rush of intense female sensuality at the knowledge that she was naked whilst Luc was fully dressed. It was so out of character for her, so alien to what she might have expected to feel, that for several seconds it had robbed her of the ability to make any kind of response to Luc's presence other than to simply lie there watching him with widened golden eyes.

Later he had told her that it had been that look of dazed wonderment in place of the angry rejection and bitterness he had expected that had encouraged him to put aside his own protective defences and show her his concern and anxiety.

'Luc...' had been all she had been able to say, in an unfamiliarly weak and hesitant voice.

'You fainted,' he told her gently, his fingers stroking her forehead in reassurance.

'I know... I haven't been well,' she responded. 'I've had some kind of flu bug...'

'Which you no doubt refused to acknowledge and fought off until it *really* made you ill,' Luc countered a little grimly.

For a moment Belle was tempted to deny what he

was saying, but the strong core of self-honesty she had developed since the failure of their marriage refused to let her.

'I had an important client meeting to attend,' she admitted. 'I should really have put it off, but this is such a cut-throat business I felt I couldn't afford to do so...'

Five years ago Belle had left the firm she had originally worked for and had set up in business on her own. Financially the rewards were not perhaps quite so high as they had been, and certainly the demands on her time and her energies were far greater, but so was the sense of satisfaction she gained from being her own boss.

Just recently, though, she found that she was deliberately ignoring opportunities to further her business and add to her client base, that she was beginning to respond to a previously unacknowledged need to allow things into her life other than her work, beginning to admit to a sense of awareness that there were certain things she was missing out on, certain emotional needs in her life which were not being met. But of course these were admissions she could not make to Luc, not when all those years ago Luc had accused her of putting her career above their marriage, when Luc had warned her that one day she would find herself lonely and alone.

'You always did make far too many demands on yourself,' Luc told her wryly, his criticism turning to concern as she suddenly started to shiver. 'You're freezing,' he told her almost accusingly.

This caused her to flash back at him, her eyes brilliant with a mixture of fever and pride, 'And whose fault is that? I'm not the one who took off my robe.'

Immediately she wished she hadn't spoken, because now Luc, who before had only been looking at her face, watching her eyes, suddenly switched his gaze to her body.

Instinctively Belle tensed her muscles.

She had been a girl when she and Luc had first met. Now she was a woman. As a girl she had taken for granted the lush femininity of her body, the luminous sheen to her skin, the softness of her female flesh. Now she was older, her body shape different.

She could see the way Luc was frowning at her. No doubt she didn't compare well to whoever was currently sharing his bed. After all, a man in his position, a man with all his sexual assets, his charisma, his good looks, not to mention his powerful position as a leader in his scholastic field, was bound to be able to have his pick of all the best of his female students.

She, on the other hand... But, no, she wasn't going to start thinking about how empty her life was, how empty it had been since their divorce... Why should she? That had been her choice. There had been men, offers, opportunities; she had simply been too picky to accept any of them.

Luc was still frowning.

'You're too thin,' he told her abruptly. 'Are you eating properly?'

'It's fashionable to be thin,' Belle returned sharply, even though she knew perfectly well that her body weight was normally a good half-stone heavier than it was right now, and that she personally had thought herself a little on the thin side before this bout of flu had brought her weight down even further.

'Fashionable!' Luc's eyebrows rose.

'Yes,' Belle persisted. 'Just because *you* don't find my body attractive, that doesn't—'

'I didn't say I didn't find you attractive. I simply said you were too thin,' Luc interrupted softly. 'As a matter of fact—'

Quite what might have happened if he hadn't abruptly stopped speaking she didn't know, but he continued, his voice oddly hoarse, 'You need something to eat. Get into bed and don't you dare move so much as a muscle whilst I go downstairs and get you something.'

But she could hazard a very strong guess, Belle reflected with self-honesty after the door had closed after him. After all, whatever might have been the cause of their final quarrel, and her pride-fuelled abandonment of their marriage, it had had nothing to do with her not finding him physically attractive, or with her not wanting him...as a man...

Her face hot, she reminded herself that she was a woman in her mid-thirties, a woman whose body, whose emotions, whose most private physical needs had never once betrayed her in all the time she had been on her own.

It must be her weakened state that was making her so vulnerable, she reassured herself. Yes, that was it. That and the shock of seeing Luc so unexpectedly, of finding herself in such an unexpectedly dangerously intimate situation with him.

Thinking of which, where on earth *was* her robe?

She had just reached the bedroom door when Luc opened it from the other side, frowning severely at her when he saw that she had disobeyed his edict.

'You shouldn't be out of bed. You've already passed out once,' he reminded her severely.

'I was looking for my robe,' Belle informed him, trying to summon what dignity she could. No small task when one was standing shivering and nude in front of the man who had every reason to find the sight of one's naked form less than physically appealing.

'Get into bed. I'll go and find it for you,' Luc told her with unexpected gentleness. 'At least you've got the sense to keep this place properly heated, even if you *don't* seem able to feed yourself. What on earth do you live on, Belle? There is hardly anything in your fridge or cupboards.'

'That's because I prefer to buy fresh food,' Belle returned quickly and loftily. 'And I've been too ill to feel like going out shopping for the last few days.'

'Mmm... Well, I've managed to find a can of soup and some eggs. Drink your soup whilst I go back down and make you an omelette.'

He was certainly behaving very masterfully, Belle acknowledged as she tucked hungrily into her soup when he had gone back to the kitchen.

But hadn't that always been one of the causes of their problems? The fact that it had irked his male pride that *she* had been the main provider. Not that he had tried to dominate her. No. She could never have loved him the way she had had he been like that. But she had always felt that he had subtly punished her for not being more helpless, more financially dependent upon him.

The warmth of her bed now that she had snuggled under the duvet and the blissful comfort of the hot soup in her stomach combined to make her feel relaxed and sleepy. So much so that by the time Luc returned with the promised omelette she was already half asleep. The sight of the amount of food he had piled onto the plate brought her sharply awake, though. Indignantly she stared at it.

'I can't eat all that,' she protested. 'It's indecent. There must be at least a dozen eggs there...'

'Not quite,' Luc told her cheerfully, without any apparent remorse. 'Actually we're *both* going to eat it. I don't care to miss out on my meals even if you do,' he told her severely. 'And since I could only find one plate, we shall have to share.'

'The others are in the dishwasher,' Belle informed him, and then added defensively, 'I'm a single woman living alone, Luc. I don't have either the space or the need to own a full twelve-place dinner service.'

'Surely you entertain sometimes?'

'Not really. I prefer to take business clients out, it's much easier and more professional. And besides—' she chewed a little betrayingly on her bottom lip '—it isn't always a good idea to invite male clients into one's home...'

'You've had problems with men...clients...behaving badly towards you?' Luc demanded fiercely.

'Er...it was a long time ago, when we first divorced and it was probably my own fault. I didn't realise the false message I could be giving inviting a client home.'

'He frightened you? Hurt you? Who...?'

'Nothing like that,' Belle hastened to assure him. 'It was just that there was a rather...embarrassing episode. A misunderstanding, really, that was all.'

'You mean one of your clients tried to...?'

'I've told you, Luc, it was all a long time ago, and fortunately he accepted that there'd been a misunderstanding. But after that I made the decision not to invite clients home—not that the way I run my life, either private or professional, is any business of yours.'

'Don't you ever find it lonely living alone?' he asked her, completely throwing her. But before she could make the defensively protective denial that was hovering on her lips he further confounded her by admitting quietly, 'I know that I do...'

'You...you live alone...?' Belle raised her eyes to his face.

'I've lived alone since you left,' he told her simply.

Belle's appetite had completely deserted her, and oddly Luc didn't seem to be particularly hungry either.

'Belle...'

'Luc...'

'I'm glad to see you kept the bedhead,' he told her huskily, and then he lifted his hand and reached past her to trace the initials and the date he had carved into it. 'I have to admit it isn't anywhere near so handsome, though, as the one you bought.'

'Nor so expensive,' Belle said quietly, dropping

her gaze from his so that he wouldn't guess that the cost she *was* referring to was not in terms of the money she had spent on the bedhead, but the reckless wastage, the dreadful continuing payment with increasingly heavy interest she was still having to make in terms of broken dreams and lost love.

'Belle...'

As he withdrew his hand from the bedhead and straightened up, Belle lifted her head.

His gaze met hers and held it. Her whole body started to tremble, her heart beating far too fast.

Luc started to lower his head towards hers. He was going to kiss her. Belle just knew it. Her heart was racing so fast that she thought it might explode. Automatically she closed her eyes. She could almost feel the warmth of Luc's mouth against her own, taste the wonderful familiarity of his kiss, breathe in his special scent, feel...

'I must go...'

Abruptly her eyes snapped open. Luc *wasn't* going to kiss her after all.

'It was very thoughtful of you to call,' she told him stiffly. 'I'll get in touch with Carol and tell her about Great-Aunt Alice's mistake.'

'It's quite a coincidence that your niece and my cousin should be marrying...'

'Yes...I suppose it is.'

'Andy was telling me the last time I saw him that he's applied to finish his training in the same town where Joy has just been appointed a junior registrar at the local hospital.'

Immediately Belle guessed what he must be thinking.

'And of course you don't approve of that. No doubt you think *she* should be the one to follow *him*?'

'On the contrary,' Luc replied evenly. 'I think that he's a very fortunate young man to have a woman who loves him so much that she's prepared to take on the burden of being the major wage-earner until he's fully qualified. After all, if Andy hadn't changed his mind about the career path he wanted to follow, he would be qualified himself by now.

'I still think it's ironic that it takes longer to train to be a vet than a doctor, but I hope that Andy will appreciate both Joy and her love, and that he doesn't allow his male pride—'

He broke off and looked away from her. 'Fortunately his generation has a far healthier and more flexible attitude towards interchanging the traditional roles than ours perhaps did.'

Belle tried to speak, but found that she couldn't articulate a single word because of the lump in her throat.

This was the first time Luc had ever acknowledged that he could have been wrong. She *knew* that *she* had made mistakes, gone about things the wrong way, been rather less careful of his male pride than she might have been, but this was the first time she had felt that Luc, too, might have regrets, doubts about the things he had done, the way he had behaved…reacted. Perhaps if she had known that then…if they had sat down together like this then and talked… But Luc wasn't sitting down now; he was getting up. He was going away—leaving her— his Good Samaritan duties done.

Belle watched as he walked towards the door.

'Thank you for...for the soup,' she told him gruffly as he opened it, and then she looked away, closing her eyes, unable to bear watching him go out of her life...again...

When several seconds went by and she hadn't heard the final click of the door she opened her eyes again, widening them as she saw how close Luc was to the bed. How close he was to her.

'You don't have to thank me Belle—not ever—not for *anything*,' he told her, and then he did what he hadn't done before. He bent his head and kissed her.

A brief, non-sexual, amicable little kiss—or so he'd said it was supposed to be, when he'd told her later—but somehow their lips, their mouths, their senses had other ideas, and the brief brush of his cool mouth against hers became something warmer, deeper...longer...and far, far more intimate as their mouths clung together.

'I shouldn't be doing this. You're not well,' Luc groaned, but he still took her in his arms, holding her tightly against his heart so that she could feel its fierce thud as he cupped her face in his hands and looked deeply into her eyes.

Very tenderly Luc caressed her lips with his. Somewhere in the distance Belle could hear a noise, shrill, intrusive, unwanted. Her telephone was ringing. Reluctantly she broke the kiss.

'It's Carol,' she told Luc as she recognised her sister's number on the visual display unit.

When she picked up the receiver she could hear her sister's voice announcing frantically, 'Belle, something dreadful's happened. Great-Aunt Alice has sent...'

Belle could see Luc walking towards the door. She wanted to call out to him to stay...not to go...not to leave her. But she was a grown woman, and grown women did not give in to such foolish urges, such foolish emotions.

Covering the receiver, she called out instead, 'I'm afraid I'm going to have to ask you to let yourself out...'

'Belle? Belle, is someone there with you?' she could hear Carol demanding curiously.

'It was just...an unexpected visitor...' Belle responded as casually as she could as Luc closed the bedroom door very gently behind himself.

And it was, after all, the truth.

Carol, at any rate, seemed perfectly happy with her explanation, continuing urgently, 'I don't know *how* to tell you this, but Great-Aunt Alice has only gone and sent your wedding invitation to Luc. Belle! Belle, are you still there?'

'I'm still here,' Belle confirmed.

Ten minutes later, after her sister had rung off, Belle warned herself sternly that there was no point in wondering or dwelling on what might have happened if her sister hadn't rung up, if Luc had continued to kiss her, if she had actually dared to give in to the emotions, the sensations that had been flooding her.

With Luc's lips caressing hers it had been extraordinarily easy to forget their quarrels and the harsh words they had said to one another in the final, agonising dying throes of their marriage and oh, so easy to remember instead the love they had once shared.

Had *once* shared?

Shakily Belle closed her eyes. It must be the weakening effect of her flu that was making her feel like this, making her remember...regret...wish... But the way she had felt just now, when Luc had kissed her, had been the reaction of the woman she was now to the man he was now, she acknowledged with painful honesty. She had wanted him as the man he was, had felt that age-old female response to his nearness and his touch as the woman she had grown into.

Not wanting to pursue such a dangerous train of thought, Belle punched her pillow and told herself that she ought to be trying to sleep and get herself better.

Belle was asleep when Luc let himself back into her small house several hours later. He had found her spare keys hanging on a hook in the kitchen, neatly labelled. He had been reluctant to leave her on her own, having seen how ill she looked. She was far too thin, far too pale, and no doubt she was working far too hard and neglecting to look after herself properly.

A wry smile curled his mouth. One of her complaints about him had been that he fussed too much.

'When I'm hungry, I'll eat,' had been her standard response to him in the old days, when he had complained about their lack of ordered meal times.

These days he could sympathise more with that view. He certainly found no pleasure in going home to an empty house and cooking for himself, and as a consequence he found that he tended to snatch meals on the run between lectures and meetings. But at least he could dine in hall if he wanted to—the academic's version of the businessman's 'business lunches', he acknowledged ruefully as he climbed the stairs and went into Belle's kitchen to unpack the groceries he had bought whilst he was out.

No doubt she would be furious with him for what she would undoubtedly consider to be his unwarranted interference. But, deny it though she would, there was still, on his part at least, a sense of there being a bond between them, a relationship, and he could no more have returned to Cambridge after his meeting with fellow academics without returning to check that she was all right than he could have walked away when she'd opened the door to him and he had seen how ill she looked.

It was true that all those years ago, after the initial shock, and his instinctive attempt to deny what was happening, he had been forced to acknowledge that, given the growing frequency and intensity of their quarrels, and the disharmony between them, he'd had no option but to accept Belle's decision that she wanted a divorce. Certainly it had seemed impossible at the time for them to be able to reconcile their growing differences, but in the years since then his position had given him plenty of opportunity to observe and consider the changes taking place in the way the sexes related to one another and ran their relationships.

It was no extraordinary thing at all now for a female student to take on the financial responsibility of helping to support her partner, or to go on to become the main breadwinner whilst he opted to continue his studies; why, even some of his female colleagues were openly outspoken about the fact that they, as highly qualified women earning good salaries, actively *preferred* to have a partner who was happy to take a more passive but nevertheless extremely important and supportive role in their relationship.

'It's just too exhausting battling to accommodate two major egos,' one female colleague had told him frankly, when they had been discussing the subject. 'Quite honestly, whilst there's a part of me that will always be drawn to the high-powered "Alpha"-type male biologically speaking, as a thinking woman, I *know* that I have a far better chance of happiness and a far pleasanter life with a man who is prepared to let me take the lead role.'

Not that he and Belle's relationship had been quite like that.

He personally had *always* considered Belle to be his equal in *every* way, although sexually she had tended to look to him to initiate their lovemaking, at least in the earlier stages of their relationship. If he was honest, Luc had to admit that his own inflexible old-fashioned male attitude to money had been the maggot which had eaten away at the foundations of their marriage. Although he had always been too proud to admit it to her, it *had* irked him, *hurt* him, that she had been the one to provide the major part of their income, and because of that he had been less than generous in sharing the pleasure it had given her to buy things for their home...and for him.

Yes, there had been faults on both sides, but...

But it was too late now to go back and rewrite the past. Not the past, maybe, but there was still the present...and the future. Luc paused in the act of closing the fridge door.

Holding Belle in his arms earlier, he had been overwhelmed by an impulse...a need...to take things further. Very thoughtfully he made his way to Belle's bedroom. She was asleep, lying curled up like a small child, looking very alone in the large bed. And she had let her guard down enough with him to imply she had not shared that bed with anyone else.

Which put them both on an equal footing.

Luc knew men who complained that the sexual frustration of being without a partner drove them to irrational excesses of behaviour and unsuitable relationships... But, desperately though he had missed Belle, and the intimacy of their lovemaking, he had never experienced any desire to fill her place with another woman, another body...any body...just to ease the sexual ache of her absence. And yet earlier today, holding her, he had been sharply and shockingly reminded of just how powerfully potent the male sex drive could be, of just how determinedly and dangerously it could overrule reason and logic.

If the intensity with which he had once wanted Belle, and loved her, had dimmed over the years, then being so close to her had certainly given him a sharp reminder of just how it had once been.

Luc sat down on the bed beside her, watching her, remembering.

The first time he had held her, really properly held her, she had literally trembled with excitement in his arms. When he had kissed her he had felt as though he had instantly become Master of the Universe, Lord of Eternity, no mere mortal any longer, at once so strong and powerful that there was nothing, no goal beyond his reach, and at the same time so achingly vulnerable that she could have reduced him to emotional dust simply by refusing him her smile.

It had been the love of poets and sages, beyond reason, beyond logic, and certainly beyond the control of a mere mathematician, and miraculously she had felt the same.

It was, they had both sworn, a love that would last for ever; they were soulmates, two perfect halves of an even more perfect whole. So why and how had they managed to destroy it? Not so much, perhaps, through human frailty, but rather through human strength, pride, arrogance, mistaken belief on the part of both of them that they were wholly in the right.

It was no doubt fitting that he should be examining the flaws which had led to the destruction of their marriage now—if not on the eve of his cousin's marriage to Belle's niece then certainly on the runway approach to it. Not that Andy was likely to ask him for his advice, or his admission on where he had gone wrong.

He was still deep in thought when Belle opened her eyes. At first she thought she was seeing a mirage. She had seen Luc leave with her own eyes, but here he was, sitting on the side of her bed as he looked towards the window, his expression, in repose, both stern and sad.

Instinctively she reached out to touch him.

Instantly he turned towards her.

'Belle, you're awake. How are you feeling?'

'Better,' she told him, dismissing the subject of her health in favour of something which interested her far more.

'What are you doing here? I thought you'd gone.'

'I had…I had a meeting to attend, otherwise… I was concerned about you. You shouldn't neglect your health, you know. You're…'

'Not getting any younger. I know,' Belle agreed dryly.

'I've bought you some groceries,' Luc informed her. 'If you're hungry.'

I'm not… Belle had been about to say, but instead—as she would be the first to admit to herself later—a little deviously she fibbed.

'Well, yes, I am a little, but I really don't feel like getting up and cooking. My head still aches and…'

'You stay right where you are,' Luc commanded her, getting up. 'I'll do the cooking.'

'Are you sure? Don't you have to get back?'

'Yes and no,' Luc told her promptly, holding her eyes as he added quietly, 'After all, what is there for me to go back to other than an empty house?

'I'll go and make us both something to eat, and then, if you feel up to it, Belle, I'd like us to talk.'

'Talk?' Steadily Belle returned his gaze, her own never faltering as she read the message he was giving her with his eyes. 'I feel up to it,' she responded huskily.

CHAPTER THREE

'BELLE, Carol says it's time for the wedding breakfast. Carol's got the reception line organised to go in. It's a shame that you won't be on the top table, but…'

'Mum, I really don't mind,' Belle reassured her mother. 'After all, I'm only Joy's aunt, not her mother or her bridesmaid…'

'I can't believe the last wedding we had in the family was yours and Luc's. I saw him earlier. He made a point of coming over to talk to your father and me…'

Belle smiled and waited patiently, knowing what was coming next. Her mother had never made any secret of the fact of how much she had liked Luc.

'I hate to say it, Belle,' she had told her younger daughter unhappily after the divorce, 'but this is what happens when a woman puts her job before her husband.'

'Mum…*I'm* the one who wanted the divorce, not Luc,' Belle had reminded her mother sharply. 'And as for putting my job first—'

She had stopped, knowing that there was no point in arguing with her mother and upsetting her. She was a woman of her time and had what Belle considered to be antiquated, old-fashioned views about a woman's role in life. She had worked as a secretary until Carol had been conceived, and after that she had stayed at home to look after her daughters and her husband. Not out of any sense of duty, but because that was what she had wanted to do.

'Carol's put you on a table with—'

'Great-Aunt Alice. I know,' Belle acknowledged, dutifully smiling at her father as he came over to join them.

Joy had opted for informal round tables for seating her wedding guests. Belle's was in the middle of the room, commanding an excellent view of the other guests, but as she approached it her eyebrows lifted slightly in amused surprise as she saw Luc standing beside the chair next to her own—the chair which should have been occupied by Belle's Great-Aunt Alice.

As she joined him, Belle cast a discreet look at the place-cards. They read 'Mrs Isabelle Crawford' and 'Mr Lucius Crawford.'

'Another demonstration of Aunt Alice's handiwork,' Belle murmured to Luc as the other guests sharing their table reacted to their joint presence with varying degrees of astonishment and confusion.

'Well, let's just say that she was certainly the inspiration for it,' Luc responded in an amused undertone.

Her eyes brimming with laughter, Belle looked at Luc. 'Where *is* Aunt Alice, by the way?' she asked him.

'Er...I *was* to have been seated with my godfather....'

'Admiral Rogers?'

'Mmm…'

'Well, I hope you aren't going to regret your moment of Machiavellian interference with Joy's table plan,' Belle warned him, 'because I'm certainly going to. People are going to think it very odd to see us seated together in apparent amity…'

'Mmm… But after all, it isn't as though this is the first time lately that we've shared a meal on… amicable terms…is it?' Luc reminded her.

'No,' Belle agreed, shaking her head at him as a secret amused smile passed between them.

It had been late in the evening when Luc had eventually left. They'd talked, but by mutual agreement they'd avoided going too deep into painful areas on this occasion. He'd cooked them both a meal, and then insisted that the two glasses of red wine he had coaxed Belle to drink would be good for her and help build her up.

'Red wine *is* good for you,' he had insisted when she had raised her eyebrows.

'And chocolates,' she had semi-mocked him as she'd popped one of the delicious hand-made truffles that were her favourites into her mouth.

'The Aztecs considered chocolate to be an aphrodisiac,' he had continued blandly. 'And I've certainly no reason to argue with that.'

Belle remembered how she had blushed—and why. Long, long before the current fad for chocolate body paint there had been a certain occasion when, as a result of a cosy winter evening spent in front of an open fire, Luc had insisted on licking away the remnants of the melted chocolate she had dropped first from her fingers and then from the vee of flesh exposed by her robe where it had fallen open.

The sizzling sensuality she had experienced beneath the lazy, deliberate brush of his tongue against her skin had driven her to a frenzy of need which had resulted in her punishing him for his slow, lingering tantalisation of her body and her senses with an equally intimate exploration of his body with her own fingers and lips.

After that, the gift of chocolates between them had possessed a special intimacy and meaning, although she had assumed when he produced them this evening that he must have forgotten this.

Now, as he looked from her mouth to her fingertips, and then back to her mouth again, Belle knew that whilst he might not have bought the chocolates to remind her of that occasion—why, after all, should he have done so?—she *had* been reminded of it, *was* being reminded of it, and extremely forcibly, by a body and a set of emotions which, no matter how strictly she had fought to control them, had never truly forgiven her for denying them, and certainly had never, ever forgotten just how intense and magical the sexual rapport between her and Luc had been.

Every day for a week after that Luc rang her to see how she was feeling.

By the third day she was back at work, unofficially, at least, working from home, her body tensing every time the telephone rang in case it was Luc calling and then, abruptly, seven days after his initial visit the calls ceased.

Belle couldn't believe how bereft she felt, or how much she missed the sound of Luc's voice, as warm and rich as dark melting chocolate, touching her senses and unleashing emotions, longings, needs, she had thought long ago safely banished.

By the end of the second day without a call from him she was reduced to virtually willing him to ring, snapping unforgivably at both her mother and her sister for telephoning her and not being him.

'You need a holiday,' her mother chided her. 'You work far too hard, darling. Which reminds me. Your father and I were wondering if you could possibly manage to house-sit for us whilst we go away. Carol would do it, but with the wedding so close...'

'Don't worry, I'll do it,' Belle confirmed. She had been thinking for some time of relocating, moving herself and her business outside London. After all, her parents weren't getting any younger. Her sister and the rest of her family were all based in Cambridgeshire, her roots were there, and certainly with the aid of modern technology she could easily work from there. Besides which...

Belle wasn't sure when she had realised she was tired of opening her eyes in the morning and only being able to see a small patch of clear sky, or when she had first had that sharp yearning for the familiar flatness of the fens, the wideness of its skies. She just knew that her city life had somehow or other lost its appeal.

It was ironic to remember now how she had berated Luc, before they had found their pretty cottage, for refusing to transfer to the LSE so that they could both be based in London.

'I'm not a city person, Belle,' he had told her quietly, looking at her. 'I want our children to grow up in the same country environment that we both enjoyed.'

Their children... It had been on the tip of Belle's tongue to remind him just how impossible it was for her to even *think* of taking time out to have one child, never mind children... But instead she had demanded tartly, 'You're running ahead a little, aren't you, Luc? I can't afford to finance a nanny as well as your studies.'

It was a comment that she had bitterly regretted once she had made it. It had shamed both of them, and she had hated herself for the look she had seen in his eyes, but the thought that Luc was already planning ahead for their family, when she felt under so much pressure at work, when she had so little time and so many responsibilities, had panicked her into lashing out verbally at him.

Now things were different. Now career women of her age, all too conscious of the fast ticking of their biological clocks, were choosing the option of children without even a permanent partner, never mind the burdens on their careers, rather than miss out on the maternal boat. She envied them the single-mindedness that enabled them to make such a decision. Perhaps her own deep-rooted belief that a child thrived best surrounded by the love of both its parents sprang from the nurturing she had received in her own very happy childhood.

But that hadn't stopped her thinking sometimes that if she and Luc had had a child—children—it might have compelled them both to work a little harder at protecting their marriage. Or, conversely, it might have led to her being a single parent, struggling to bring up a child and manage her career as well.

She had surprised herself two years before when she'd discovered how easy it was to make the decision to downsize her business life, to leave behind the hectic life she had lived for so long and set up in business on her own, on a much smaller scale, with only a handful of carefully picked clients—clients who shared her own view that with wealth came a certain moral responsibility not to abuse those who did not possess such assets.

She was proud of the way she was guiding her clients to combine sound investment and financial management with an awareness of the moral issues involved in making profits, an awareness of other people's poverty, and, increasingly now, prospective clients were approaching her because they had heard of her humanitarian beliefs and record.

Three days after Luc had last rung her, he finally telephoned.

'I don't know if you've received a copy of the wedding present list or not yet,' he began, 'but it occurred to me that if we were to club together we could potentially remove one of the larger items from the list.'

'We could, but—'

'Why don't we discuss it over dinner?' Luc interrupted her.

'I...' Belle opened her mouth to refuse, but discovered instead that her voice seemed to have deserted her.

'I've got to come down to London to see a colleague the day after tomorrow. If you're free that evening I could call for you...'

'I... Yes. Very well,' Belle agreed weakly.

Luc took her to San Lorenzo which, in itself, surprised her. Not so much because of its reputation as one of the best and most expensive restaurants in London—after all, as a Fellow he was now hardly the struggling young academic he had been when she had first met him—but because she hadn't really thought that such a high-profile society place would be to his taste. What surprised her even more, though, was the discovery that the staff knew him well enough to have remembered his name.

Sensing her surprise, Luc waited until the wine waiter had gone before explaining easily to her, 'One of my students used to insist on bringing me here for her tutorials.'

'Really?' Belle gave him an icy little smile. 'I though it was the tutor who dictated where a tutorial would take place, not the student.'

'Mmm...but this student was rather special.'

'Oh.' Belle's voice had grown even icier.

'Mmm...' Luc smiled reminiscently, apparently unaware of the frigid atmosphere Belle was generating. 'She was a second or third cousin to the owners of the restaurant, and she was working here to help finance her way through university as a mature student—'

'She was a *mature* student?' Belle interrupted him sharply.

'Well, yes...'

'How mature?' Belle demanded instantly.

'Oh…pretty mature… Around fifty or so…'

Immediately Belle started to relax, unaware of the look of wry comprehension mixed with tenderness that Luc was giving her. She had always been very passionate and, whilst not possessive, certainly inclined to be very protective of their relationship. He, on the other hand, as he openly had to admit, had been rather immaturely jealous. He re-angled his chair so that the darkly handsome young waiter who was currently studying her with burning admiration was blocked out of her view.

It was late when they finally left the restaurant, and it was Luc who commented wryly as he hailed a taxi, 'We still haven't decided about the wedding present.'

'No,' Belle agreed.

They had been too busy talking about themselves to discuss anything so mundane as the rival attractions of a washing machine or a dishwasher, the two items they had narrowed their choice down to.

'I must have made you so angry sometimes,' Belle had commented at one point during the evening, when they had been discussing the breakdown of their marriage.

'Not angry, no,' Luc had countered quickly, shaking his head and reaching across the table to take hold of her hand in both of his.

'Hurt, rejected, and even at times demeaned, yes. But angry, no! It hurt me that I couldn't afford to provide you with the material things you wanted, that *I* wasn't the one paying the mortgage, that *I* couldn't go out and order that bed you wanted…'

'You were a proud man, and I should have real-ised how much what I was doing was hurting you,' Belle had groaned remorsefully, but once again Luc had shaken his head.

'No. If I was proud then it was a false pride. My pride should have been in *you*, in what you were doing for both of us, in what we were achieving by working together.

'I made a lot of mistakes, Belle, but so far as I am concerned the biggest mistake of all was the one I made when I let you go.'

'I made mistakes as well,' was all Belle had been able to whisper in response.

Now, on the way home in the taxi, she was men-tally examining what he had said. Uncertainly she darted a glance at him. His face was turned towards the window, so that she could only see his profile. To say he regretted their divorce was one thing; to say that he still loved her was something else again.

'Have you got time to come in for a cup of cof-fee?' Belle asked him uncertainly as the taxi drew up outside her home. 'We ought to make a decision about the present.'

'Yes, of course,' Luc agreed immediately.

The flowers he had given her when he'd picked her up were in water in the kitchen. As she waited for the coffee Belle breathed in their scent, touching the petals with gentle fingers.

Luc was standing in the sitting room removing his jacket as she walked in. He glanced at his watch and then cursed.

'What is it? What's wrong?' Belle asked him.

'I've just realised that it's half past twelve, and

not half past eleven as I thought,' he told her. 'That means I've missed the last train. Never mind. I'll book myself into a hotel.'

'You can't do that,' Belle protested. 'Not at this time of night. I...you could stay here...the sofa converts into a bed and...' Uncertainly her voice trailed away. Staying here with her was probably the last thing Luc wanted to do.

But just as she was wishing that she had not spoken so impetuously, she heard him saying warmly, 'Well, if you're sure you don't mind, I *would* be very grateful.

'This reminds me of the first time you stayed over with me,' Luc told her five minutes later, when they were drinking their coffee.

'You mean the night you'd taken me to a college ball and your car wouldn't start so we had to spend the night together in your rooms?'

'Mmm...that's the one,' Luc agreed reminiscently.

As she looked hurriedly away from him Belle hoped he hadn't noticed the way she had to wrap her hands tightly around her coffee mug to stop her fingers from trembling.

That had been the first night they had actually been lovers. She had known how she felt about Luc then, of course, and she had been pretty sure that he shared her feelings, but that night had been the first night she had allowed herself to give way to those feelings.

She could still vividly remember how nervous she had felt when she had walked with Luc to his rooms. There had been no question of him deliberately contriving to have his car break down—they had discovered later that the part in question had been slowly wearing away for some time—but there had been something about the way he had held her earlier when they had been dancing, the way he had kissed her, the passion with which he had whispered to her that she was the most beautiful girl at the ball, the most beautiful girl in the whole world, that had warned her how potentially dangerous it would be for them to be alone together.

He hadn't touched her at first, explaining almost formally that since there was only one bed *he* would sleep on the floor, but then she had started to shiver, as much with nerves as cold, and he had come over to her, slipping off his dinner jacket to place it on her shoulders. The moment she had felt the warmth of his fingertips against her skin she had been lost.

The sexual tension between them even in the short time they had known one another had become increasingly hard to ignore each time they touched, kissed...*breathed*... It had been there, that night, and as her body shuddered helplessly and visibly at his touch, Belle had known that the moment had come to succumb to it.

As she'd turned towards him his jacket had slid disregarded to the floor. She'd raised her face towards him, her eyes misting with emotional tears as he'd reached out and cupped it with hands that trembled just as much as her body had done. He had started to kiss her, softly, gently, and then, abruptly, he had stopped, withdrawing his mouth from hers.

Deprived of its warm, sensuous contact, Belle had

opened her eyes to stare with uncertain questioning into his.

'I can't...' he'd begun hoarsely, and then stopped. 'I don't...'

He had closed his eyes and leaned away from her, the moonlight picking out the arch of his throat and the tensing of his jaw. His eyes had closed in some kind of male anguish. Opening his eyes, he'd looked directly at her and told her thickly, 'Belle, if I touch you now...kiss you now...it won't...I can't...it won't be gentle,' he had finally told her rawly. 'I want you too much to be able to...'

Instinctively Belle had known what he meant, what he was trying to tell her. Boldly she'd stepped towards him, and away from her virginal girlhood.

'Show me,' she'd commanded him softly. And then she had simply stood waiting, watching him.

She had known, felt the difference the moment he touched her. His fingers had burned against her skin, almost as hotly and excitingly as the look she'd seen in his eyes. But that had been nothing compared to the tension, the need, the hunger she'd felt in him when he had kissed her, his mouth almost bruising the softness of hers as he'd given way to the intensity of his passion before lifting his mouth to apologise disjointedly, touching her lips with his fingertips, telling her that he was thoughtless, selfish, that he had no right...

'Stop talking and kiss me again,' Belle had interrupted him huskily. This time she had returned his passion measure for measure, biting wantonly at his bottom lip, running her tongue-tip excitedly along the shape of his mouth, opening hers to the hot thrust of his tongue when he'd reacted to her sensuality. How long they had stood like that, kissing one another, *devouring* one another, *consuming* one another in the fierce passion of their mutual need, Belle had had no idea. She'd only known that when they finally broke apart it was with one accord, as though their every movement had been perfectly choreographed. As they'd undressed one another she'd had no sense of shyness or uncertainty; there had been no clumsiness or awkwardness, only the soft slithering sound of their clothes falling away from their bodies and then that fierce, primitive moment of mutual, visual examination, of studying one another as they'd stood clothed only in the soft shadows of Luc's room.

It had been seeing the way Luc had looked at her that had made her lift her head in pride and joyous recognition of the full power of her femininity, glorying in Luc's reaction to it and her own sense of pleasure and strength in the message his reaction had given her. She was beautiful, desirable, *loved.* She had seen all that and more in his eyes.

And she'd felt the same way about him. Very gently she'd reached out and touched him, carefully placing her lips to the hollow at the base of his throat, her hands spread out across the breadth of his chest.

Very delicately she had breathed in the scent of his skin, and then very deliberately she had tasted him.

Her touch had had the effect of smashing the barrier holding back an oceanic dam, but she had given herself willingly, gladly, voluptuously and joyously

to the tumult, making herself a part of its power. Later, exhausted, beached, bleached dry, light-
headed with the release and emotionally intoxicated
with the euphoria of their love, they'd promised one
another that this was just the beginning, the explo-
sive starburst of a whole new universe of love that
they would share for ever.

The following morning she had woken up in
Luc's bed with Luc's dinner jacket draped over her
naked body. On the empty pillow beside her had
been a red rose, and attached to its stem had been
an engagement ring...

She glanced instinctively now at her left hand,
and realised to her chagrin that Luc had done the
same.

'You're still wearing it,' he told her softly, not
just echoing her thoughts but showing, too, that he
had guessed just what she had been remembering.

'It's a little bit on the tight side, and I'd have had
to have had it cut off,' she told him, not quite truth-
fully. But there was no way she was going to admit
to him just *how* she still came to be wearing it, no
way she was going to tell him about that night, less
than a year after their divorce had become final, the
night which had been the anniversary of the night
he had given the ring to her when, overcome by
sentiment and longing, she had slipped it back onto
her finger and had left it there. No need, either, to
mention just how often in times of anxiety and stress
she touched it, twisting it, gaining comfort from its
presence and from the memories she had learned to
cherish.

'Besides, *you* still wear your wedding ring,' she

pointed out, gesturing to the plain gold band on his left hand.

'*I* wasn't the one who wanted a divorce,' he told her sombrely.

'It's getting late,' Belle told him hurriedly. 'We ought to go to bed—' She stopped, and bent her head so that the thick cascade of her hair fell across her face, concealing its hot colour.

'I...I haven't anything I can offer you to wear, I'm afraid,' she apologised. 'I'll just go and get some clean towels and some bedlinen.

She kept the duvet for the sofa bed in the top of the wardrobe in her own bedroom. It was, after all, seldom used. She was standing on her dressing table stool trying to get it down when Luc saw what she was doing and came in to help her.

'Let me do that. You might fall,' he chided her.

'No, I won't,' Belle denied, and of course promptly did, bringing the duvet with her, so that as Luc rushed forward to catch her it unfurled, engulfing them both.

She was wearing a silk jersey black dress she had bought in Italy, very plain in design and very fluidly sexy. As she tumbled it rode up, revealing the soft flesh of her thigh and the wispily brief briefs she was wearing underneath.

Luc, who had put out his hand to steady her, discovered that instead of touching her waist his hand was actually resting on the smoothly naked flesh of her leg.

Were his fingertips actually stroking her skin, not just touching it? Belle wondered dizzily. Or was she just imagining it, *wanting* it...

'Belle.'

She heard him whisper her name, and instinctively she looked up at him.

'You haven't changed,' he told her softly. 'You still do things to me that…' He groaned rawly under his breath as he leaned over her. Belle felt her stomach muscles clench as she recognised that he was going to kiss her. But she didn't do anything to try to stop him. On the contrary…

'Belle…'

'Mmm….' Dreamily Belle opened her eyes at the same time as she snuggled deeper into Luc's arms.

'You know what's going to happen if we stay here like this, don't you?' Luc warned her.

'No,' Belle fibbed untruthfully as she delicately nuzzled the deliciously Luc-scented skin just below his jaw. 'But you could always show me,' she added helpfully, and encouragingly, just in case he hadn't quite got the message.

'Don't tempt me,' Luc told her throatily as he tasted the soft sweetness of her lips, deliberately lingering over them, teasing the warm outline of them with tiny little kisses.

'No, I won't tempt you,' Belle agreed obediently as she opened her mouth to the delicate probing of his tongue-tip.

Some time later, as he carried her to her bed… *their* bed…Luc reproved her, 'Didn't your mother ever tell you that it's wrong to tell lies?'

But Belle's only reply was a long, shuddering sigh of pleasure as he placed her naked body onto the bed and then covered it with his own.

'Oh, Luc… *Luc*… I've missed you so much,' she whispered to him as she held him tightly.

'Nowhere near as much as I've missed you,' he told her. 'Nowhere near…'

CHAPTER FOUR

'PEOPLE are talking about us. I warned you that they would,' Belle told Luc, shaking her head reprovingly at him as he offered her the last of the petits fours. 'Your parents have been watching us very suspiciously for the last hour.'

'Mmm...' Luc responded. 'And so have yours.'

'Well, you've got to admit it *is* rather unusual for a divorced couple to be so...'

'Intimate with one another?' Luc suggested as she finally gave in and took the sweet he was lifting to her lips.

'*Friendly* with one another, I was going to say,' Belle corrected him sternly.

'Friendly!' Luc gave her an extremely wicked look. '*You* were rather more than friendly last night...'

Quickly Belle placed her fingertip to his lips.

'Don't you dare,' she warned him. 'Don't you *dare*.' But there was laughter and warmth in her eyes, rather than disapproval, and there was a matching warmth in Luc's.

'Darling...what on earth is going on? Luc's mother has just asked me how long you and Luc have been back on speaking terms, and I must say...'

'We decided it was time we put aside our differences,' Belle told her mother calmly, half an hour later.

'Well, yes...that's very sensible, darling, but I must say...'

'Carol wants you, Mum,' Belle warned her mother as she saw her elder sister frantically beckoning to their mother, smiling to herself as she quickly escaped from her parent's anxious questions. There was no doubt about it, she and Luc *had* created quite a stir. She could see the open speculation in people's eyes as they watched them. Only Joy, the bride, seemed oblivious to the undercurrents and speculation sweeping through the room.

'Aunt Belle, there you are. I just wanted to tell you again how grateful Andy and I are to you and Luc for your wonderful wedding present. I never expected...'

'You like it, then?' Belle asked her niece with a smile.

'Like it? We are over the moon. I never...I didn't even know you knew I wanted...'

'Your mother happened to mention that you'd seen it and fallen in love with it,' Belle informed her niece fondly.

'Yes. I had...*we* had. But for you and Luc...' She stopped and fell silent as Belle raised a quizzical eyebrow.

'Well, I suppose in a way it made sense for the two of you to give us a *joint* present,' Joy acknowledged breezily. 'After all you were once... Well, anyway, we're both thrilled with it. 'I'd always loved the one that you and Luc—' She stopped awkwardly. 'Oh, dear!!'

'It's all right, darling, I fully understand what you're trying to say,' Belle reassured her.

'Oh, Andy,' Joy exclaimed thankfully as her new husband walked up. 'I was just telling Aunt Belle how thrilled we are with the present she and Luc gave us…'

'The bed? Too true. Joy had been dragging me over to that shop virtually every week.'

'I was so upset when the shop told me that it had been sold, even though I knew *we* couldn't afford it, and then when Luc came round and told me…'

'What was all that about?' Luc asked Belle, arriving back at their table as the bridal couple moved on to talk to some of their other wedding guests.

Whilst he handed Belle the drink he had gone to fetch for her she explained.

'They were thanking me…*us*…for their wedding present.'

'The bed?'

'The bed,' Belle agreed.

As he bent towards her Luc murmured provocatively, 'Well, if they get as much…pleasure out of using it as we have recently done ours…'

'Luc,' Bell warned him, and then added dryly, 'And you certainly weren't saying that when we divorced seven years ago.'

'That was then. I've come to see that shop-bought bed in a different light since then,' Luc told her suavely. 'A *very* different light…especially since you've bought those new curtains for the cottage. What was wrong with the old ones?'

'They were looking worn and tired. They were the same ones I put up before we divorced...'

'They reminded me of you,' Luc told her tenderly. 'That's why I kept them...'

'Watch out, here comes your mother,' Belle warned him.

'Luc...and Belle. You're looking wonderful, my dear...'

As she bent to kiss her ex-mother-in-law, Belle acknowledged that she had always got on well with Luc's mother, even if originally she had been a little in awe of her.

'What's this about you both giving Joy and Andrew a bed? And from the same place where— I should have thought...but then...'

'We've decided the time has come to forgive the bed its sins,' Luc told his mother mock gravely. 'After all, it wasn't entirely to blame.'

'Oh, Luc...if you're going to be flippant. I simply meant that I thought it was rather odd you should have chosen to give them something that wasn't even on their wedding list...and to give it to them jointly.'

'We decided that we could give them something a little more substantial if we combined our resources,' Belle told her gently.

'Well, yes, of course. But people do keep asking questions.'

'Perhaps we made the wrong decision,' Belle suggested.

There was a small, intimate pause, and then Luc responded obliquely, 'Oh, I don't think so.'

Belle remembered them making the decision to buy the bed, and the phone call which pre-dated it...

'Belle, I've had an idea...'

As she cradled the telephone receiver Belle felt a small frisson of pleasure begin to curl through her body. She had been away on business for three days, and it had been heaven to come home to find Luc's messages on her answering machine. And now here he was, ringing her to welcome her home.

'Mmm...?'

'About the wedding present...'

'Mmm...?'

'You did say you were coming home to house-sit for your parents this weekend, didn't you?'

'Mmm...'

'Well...'

When he'd finished telling her his idea, she exclaimed, 'You're saying that we should buy them a *bed*? Like the one we...I... It wasn't on their list.'

'No, I know, but Andy let slip that Joy would love to have one.'

'Well, yes, but, Luc! You don't think it would be tempting history to repeat itself, do you...?'

There was a small pause before Luc replied, 'Don't be silly. Besides, I thought we'd agreed.'

'It will cause talk—you know that, don't you? You and I giving them a joint gift.'

'I don't mind—let them talk,' Luc told her softly, adding persuasively, 'Andy says Joy's set her heart on the bed. It would be a wonderful surprise for Joy if we gave it to them. Andy's promised to keep it a secret from her.'

'Well, yes, I know what you're saying, and it would be lovely to surprise Joy with it.' Belle gave in.

'Yes, it would,' Luc agreed, and then asked her softly, 'What time this weekend are you expecting to arrive?'

'Belle, it's Carol. Look, I was wondering, since you're in Cambridgeshire for the next week, if you'd like to come round and have supper with us on Saturday evening. I'm not sure what time you're due to arrive, but I know that Mum and Dad are planning to leave for the airport at two in the afternoon. It would give us a chance to talk. I've been so busy with the wedding arrangements—'

'Carol, I have to go,' Belle interrupted her sister firmly. 'I'd love to see you whilst I'm down at Mum and Dad's house-sitting, but I'm afraid that Saturday night is going to be out.'

Deliberately she didn't offer any further explanation, swiftly ending the call before her sister could question her any further. There was no way she was going to tell Carol that the reason she couldn't accept her invitation was because she had already accepted an earlier one—from Luc.

And fortunately her sister was too preoccupied to question the deeply unusual circumstances of Belle and Luc giving Joy and Andy a joint wedding present.

From the sitting room window of her parents' house, Belle could see a car pulling into the drive. She drew

in a sharp breath as she saw Luc climbing out of it
and walking towards the front door.

'What are you doing here?' she demanded as she
opened the door to him. 'You said you'd pick me
up at eight o'clock tonight...'

'I know, but I couldn't wait any longer to see
you,' Luc confessed as she let him in. 'Oh, Belle...'

Not since they had been a courting couple had
they behaved like this, Belle acknowledged as Luc
barely waited until he had closed the front door behind them to take her hungrily in his arms and kiss
her with a passion which she admitted she had no
difficulty whatsoever in matching.

'It's less than a week since you saw me,' Belle
managed to find the logic to remind him when she
was finally able to talk.

'A lifetime,' Luc told her mock solemnly, his tone
belying the look of sparkling humour in his eyes.

This was a side of him she had never truly appreciated in the past, Belle acknowledged, as she
shared his laughter, his sense of fun and teasing
good humour. Perhaps because she had taken herself
so seriously in those days, she had never allowed
herself to appreciate it, but, as she was now discov-
ering, shared laughter was a very, very potent aphrodisiac.

'Carol rang the other day. She wanted me to have
dinner with *them* this evening.'

'What did you tell her?' Luc asked as he followed
her into her parents' kitchen.

'I said that I'd got a prior engagement,' Belle informed him wryly.

'A prior *engagement*...mmm...'

There was no mistaking the way Luc reinforced the word 'engagement', and followed it with a meaningful look at her left hand.

'Luc, honestly!' Belle reproved him. 'What on earth would people think if they could see us…hear you…?'

'I don't care what other people think…only what *you* think…what *you* feel,' Luc told her extravagantly.

'Oh, Luc…' A little shakily Belle went into his arms. 'Are we right to be behaving like this? We made a mistake once…'

'Look, we promised ourselves that we wouldn't question what was happening, that we'd just take things…and each other…on trust,' Luc reminded her.

'Yes, I know,' she admitted. 'It's just… Mmm… Luc, someone might see us,' she protested half-heartedly as he started to kiss her.

'Mmm…but at least this time it won't be your father,' Luc responded reminiscently. 'Remember that evening when he came down?'

'Mmm…he hadn't realised that you'd come in with me, and he walked into the kitchen, where I'd gone to make us both a cup of coffee…'

'And I'd followed you to help you.'

'Oh, that was what you were doing, was it?' Belle asked darkly.

'Well, at least this time there's no chance of your father walking in,' Luc commented, taking her back in his arms.

Several bliss-filled seconds later, Belle was just

snuggling deeper into his embrace when the back door suddenly opened.

'Belle, it's me, Jane...' she heard her mother's friend and neighbour calling out cheerfully.

Any hopes that she and Luc had managed to spring apart without being seen were squashed when she heard Jane's voice change completely as she started to apologise in a flustered voice. 'Oh, dear, I'm sorry, I hadn't realised...' And then it changed again as she recognised Luc. 'Luc... But what...?'

'Luc called round to see Mum and Dad,' Belle fabricated quickly. 'He hadn't realised that they'd gone away.' Heavens, it was amazing how very creative one could be with the truth when the need arose, and she wasn't even blushing.

'Oh, I see...'

Uncertainly she looked from Belle to Luc, and then back again.

'How's your eye now, Belle?' Luc asked solicitously. 'She'd got an eyelash in it,' he told Jane straight-faced.

'Oh...I see... Well, I only called round to say hello,' Jane explained. 'Er...I'll er...leave you to it...'

'Now the whole neighbourhood is going to know that you were here,' Belle groaned after she had gone. 'Oh, Luc...'

'Oh, Belle...'

'Now what are you doing?' she demanded a little breathlessly as he took her back in his arms.

'Looking for that eyelash,' Luc told her.

'I just hope that Jane hasn't seen us driving away together,' Belle worried half an hour later as Luc backed his car out of her parents' drive.

'We've got a perfectly legitimate excuse for being seen together. We're buying Joy and Andy a joint wedding present—remember?'

'Yes, I know that, but we're not doing that now, are we?'

'No, we're not doing it now,' Luc agreed urbanely.

'So where *are* we going?' Belle asked him curiously ten minutes later. 'It's too early for dinner and...'

'Wait and see.'

As they passed the country church where her niece was to be married, Belle leant forward in her seat.

'Does it bring back memories?' Luc asked her.

'Yes,' Belle admitted.

They had been married there themselves, and her eyes blurred briefly with emotional tears as she remembered how deliriously happy she had been, how filled with excitement mingled with awe at the thought of marrying Luc.

Not that she had originally wanted a big white wedding with all the trimmings. She had wanted something far quieter and more intimate.

It had been Luc who had persuaded her otherwise, pointing out to her that the vows they made to one another would be just as precious no matter where they made them, and that it would be unfair of them to exclude their families from the occasion.

'You wanted to be married somewhere private and out in the open air—remember?'

'Yes, I do,' Belle agreed, her voice a little husky with emotion at the way he had picked up on her own thoughts. 'An island, or the top of a hill... I wanted our marriage to be different, special... romantic, a private memory we could cherish for ever...'

'I know.'

'Instead it was a full family affair with me in a dress like a meringue and eight bridesmaids.'

'You looked beautiful.'

'You could barely get close enough to kiss me after the vicar had said you could because of the width of my dress hoops. Remember?'

Luc started to laugh.

'It wasn't funny,' Belle protested indignantly. 'A bride whose groom can't kiss her is no laughing matter.'

'I wasn't laughing at that,' Luc told her. 'I was just remembering the panic we had when no one could find little Timmy and then he crawled out from underneath your skirt.'

Belle laughed too.

'Yes, he'd been under the table whilst I was talking to his parents and he'd crawled under my hoops without any of us noticing.'

Silently they exchanged reminiscent looks, and then out of the corner of her eye Belle saw a familiar signpost.

'You're taking me home?' she asked Luc incredulously, not realising until it was too late just how betraying her choice of words had been.

'I'm taking you home,' Luc agreed huskily.

This time the silence between them was deeper,

closer, and potentially tense with unspoken emotion. Belle could feel her heart starting to beat far too fast as they drove through the village and Luc took the narrow country lane that led to the house they had bought together.

Belle had fallen in love with it at first sight, and the feelings that swamped her as they rounded the bend and she saw the house through its framing protective canopy of trees made her press her lips firmly together to stop her chin from wobbling and trembling. They had bought this house with such love and she had left it in so much pain that she could hardly bear to remember just how she had felt.

'It hasn't changed,' Belle whispered as Luc stopped the car.

Originally two separate farmworkers' cottages, the pair had been knocked through into one when they had bought it, and the whole building carefully renovated.

It was surrounded by a large garden overlooking the lane at the front and running down to a stream at the rear. Inside the front door was a long, narrow stone-flagged hallway and a flight of steep stairs. The stone mullioned windows gave the house character and an air of timelessness.

'Oh, you've still got the same curtains,' was the only thing she could think of to say as Luc helped her out of the car.

She had bought the material on impulse one wet afternoon when Luc had been studying and she had driven into Cambridge to do some shopping.

She had found the heavy damask fabric by accident on a market stall. It had come originally from one of the colleges, the stall owner had told her.

Uncertainly Belle had fingered the rich heavy fabric. Even at the stall holder's price it was still horribly expensive, but it was also perfect for the house.

She reminded herself that only the previous week she and Luc had rowed about money, and in retaliation for his claim that their expenses were far too high she had immediately accused him of spending far too much on the books he had claimed he needed to study.

'I thought that's what college libraries were for,' she had told him scornfully, still smarting from his reference to the fact that she had spent more on a pair of luxury tights then he had done on a whole week's lunches.

'It is, but they don't carry a set of these,' Luc had countered quietly.

So she had walked determinedly away from the stall, only to walk back again ten minutes later, closing her eyes as she told the woman she would have the fabric.

She had made the curtains herself. How could she preach economy to Luc and then pay someone else to make them?

'They're beautiful,' Luc had told her quietly once they were hung, but the lack of genuine enthusiasm in his voice had hurt and angered her.

If she wanted to spend the money she had worked so hard to earn on expensive curtains, then she had every right to do so. And she had told him so.

Remembering the incident now, Belle winced at

her own careless disregard of Luc's feelings, her lack of wisdom and foresight.

'The shop has sent me a brochure with photographs of the different styles of beds they do,' Luc explained as he unlocked the front door and ushered Belle in in front of him. 'Since they don't carry a stock of each design, I thought you might want to look at it.'

'Do they still do our bed?'

'"Our" bed?' Luc gave her a slow, teasing smile. 'It's *my* bed now—remember? The removal men took the one I made when you moved out. Of course it's not too late for us to—'

'No, no, I don't want—I'm keeping the bed I've got,' Belle told him quickly, and then added a little defensively, 'I like it, I'm used to it—it's...'

It's a tiny bit of you, she could have said.

Belle shot Luc a slightly self-conscious look, but he was already ushering her towards the drawing room.

'Come and sit down. I'll make us both a cup of tea and then you can look at the brochure.'

The sitting room was just as she had left it. The covers on the sofas a little faded, perhaps, and the rust carpet's original colour softened by the sun, but the classic timelessness of the furniture Belle had chosen because the house had demanded it had stood the passage of time very well, she acknowledged.

Luc might not have changed anything, but she could see that the room had been repainted at some stage and its surfaces were dust-free and well polished.

'Sorry about the delay,' he apologised ten minutes later, when he reappeared with their tea and the catalogue. 'I couldn't find this. Mrs Leyton, who comes in from the village to clean for me a couple of times a week, had "tidied" it away.'

Being in the house which had once been her home, the home she had once shared with Luc, who was here beside her, whose home it still was, was causing her to feel so many conflicting emotions that Belle could barely concentrate on the brochure he was showing her.

Certainly the company had extended its original small range of furniture, and the four-poster beds they had added to their list were works of art—and had she been looking for a new bed—

But they weren't looking for a bed for the master bedroom here; they were looking for one for Joy and Andy. And since they already knew exactly which one they wanted...

'I really ought to get back,' Belle told Luc hurriedly, closing the brochure. 'But first I need to go upstairs and wash my hands...'

One of the drawbacks to the house had been the fact that it had not possessed a downstairs cloakroom. They had had plans to add one at the same time as they added an extra bedroom suite. Confidently Belle made her way upstairs whilst Luc carried their tea things back to the kitchen.

Up here, too, nothing seemed to have changed. The dried flowers she had arranged were gone from the deep window on the landing, but the curtains were the same, and... On her way to the bathroom she suddenly paused, stopped, and then retraced her steps.

The door to the master bedroom was closed. Very gently she turned the handle and then stepped inside.

It was like stepping back in time to another world. Once inside the bedroom she had shared with Luc the memories came flooding back with such force that she had to cling to the door for support. It was in this room that they had loved, laughed and fought. Belle could hardly bear now to think of the sacrilege it had been to fight in a room which should have known only the intimate content of their love.

Shakily she let go of the door and walked over to the bed, her hand trembling as she automatically smoothed the creases out of Luc's side of the duvet.

Luc's side...

Unwanted and unheralded the tears came hot and fast, a silent glissade of pain and regret. Her body shook with the force of her sobs, but still she didn't make a sound.

'Belle?'

Shocked, she stiffened her body in rejection of the warmth of Luc's arms. She hadn't heard him come in, didn't want him to see her like this.

'You're crying,' he told her, begging rawly as he turned her round to face him, 'Don't...please, don't.'

'Oh, Luc, I feel so ashamed when I remember the things I did...the things I said,' Belle wept, unable to conceal what she was feeling. 'I was so thoughtless, so selfish...'

'No more thoughtless or selfish than I was stubborn and unreasonable,' Luc comforted her.

'It's all such a waste,' Belle cried heartbrokenly.

'Love is never wasted,' Luc told her softly. 'Just like it never dies…'

Belle looked up at him.

'It's not too late for us, Belle, we still have the future…*our* future…together—if we choose to take it…'

'What are you saying?' she whispered. 'We said that we wouldn't rush things or make promises, that we'd take each day as it comes…'

'I know, but I know as well that each day isn't going to be enough for me. I want all your days. All *our* days.'

'Remember Cheringham House?' he asked her obliquely.

Belle nodded her head. The stately Georgian property was owned by the local council and had been painstakingly renovated and opened to the public. She had always loved it, often coaxing Luc away from his studies to go round it with her.

'Under the new law, it's now been given permission to hold weddings. It has an island…'

'In the middle of the lake with a pretty mock-Gothic temple… Yes, I know,' Belle agreed.

And then, as she looked at him, she breathed, 'Oh, Luc, we couldn't…could we?'

Ten minutes later, when she had finally extracted herself from his arms, she reminded him, 'We're supposed to be going out to dinner, remember?'

'I've got a better idea,' Luc told her masterfully. 'Why don't we eat here…?'

'Here?'

Belle looked at him.

'What are we going to eat?' she asked him shakily.

'I know what I want to eat,' Luc responded sensually. 'All right, all right,' he acknowledged as he fielded the look she gave him. 'Let's go down and see what we can find in the freezer.'

'Mmm...champagne and lobster. You really are spoiling me,' Belle told Luc contentedly as she licked her fingers.

'Well, I have to admit it was a lucky find. I'd forgotten all about the lobster. It was a present...'

'From one of your students?' Belle asked a little possessively, a warning glint in her eyes.

Luc laughed.

'No, from my mother, as it happens.'

Belle allowed herself to relax. His mother was a wonderful cook, and loved nothing better than passing on the results of her skills to her friends and family.

'Mmm...that was wonderful,' Belle declared, stretching sensuously.

'Mmm...wonderful,' Luc agreed, reaching across to slide his hand into the tempting vee of flesh exposed by the borrowed shirt she was wearing and bending his head to kiss her.

'Just think,' he murmured as he covered her mouth with his, 'if we bought a four-poster, we could close the curtains and eat in bed in true Tudor fashion.'

'Throwing the bones out for the dogs and serfs, you mean?' Belle teased back, wrinkling her nose as she disagreed. 'Yuck, I don't think so. Although I must admit the idea of a four-poster does have a certain amount of appeal...'

'Mmm...although I have to say that there is something deliciously sensual about the way the light from the window touches your skin which I couldn't enjoy through closed curtains.'

'Luc...' Belle reproved unsteadily as he gently pushed his shirt back off her shoulders, exposing her breasts to the early evening sunlight streaming in through the windows, and then moved back to enjoy the results of his handiwork.

'Your skin looks as though it's been sprinkled with gold dust,' he told her softly. 'You have the most beautiful skin, Belle, the most beautiful body...'

'I'm thirty-four,' Belle protested, but in truth she thought that Luc's body looked even more sensually exciting now than it had done when they were younger. Perhaps Luc was right in what he had said to her earlier, that it took pain and loss and despair to make one appreciate love properly.

Well, she had certainly experienced all of those. They both had.

She trembled a little with excited anticipation as Luc's hands cupped her breasts. Her body was so intensely responsive to him it frightened her a little.

He kissed her throat and then her nipples, his eyes darkening as he looked back into her face.

'I don't know how I managed to live without you,' he told her rawly, and then added, 'But it wasn't really living; it was simply existing.'

His mouth returned to her breasts, teasing their

hard crests. Belle moaned eagerly beneath her breath and reached for him. Her need for him overwhelmed her, urgent, immediate and hotly demanding. The feel of his weight against her body, between her thighs, made her shudder wildly. Her hands clasped his back, her nails pressed hard against his skin as she clung passionately to him. She cried out as he entered her, a wild, elemental cry of love and need mingled with pain and regret for all that they had lost, all that she had thrown away, and then the past was forgotten, the future just a shadowy vision, the only thing that mattered the thrusting movement of his body within hers.

Luc cried out fiercely against her as his own need peaked and her body exploded into a frantic spiral of orgasmic pleasure.

Damp, panting, her heart still racing, Belle looked up into his eyes.

'Great-Aunt Alice could have an awful lot to answer for,' she warned him meaningfully. 'This wasn't something I'd planned for...'

'All the more reason to take that trip to Cheringham House just as soon as we can, then,' Luc responded.

'I might not——' Belle began, but Luc shook his head, and then bent it and kissed her tenderly.

'With or without child, I want you back in my life, Belle.' Belle snuggled closer to him and then tensed.

'Luc, I don't want to have to tell anyone about us...not yet...it's too soon. What we have between us is too...precious. I...'

'I understand,' Luc confirmed as he kissed her again.

'Belle.'

Belle gave Luc an answering smile as he called her name and cut a swathe through the busy fellow wedding guests to reach her side.

'What happened?' he asked her quietly, adding with a rueful look, 'I was just beginning to wonder if I ought to send my mother on a search party to the Ladies for you.'

'It's just as well that you didn't,' Belle whispered, glancing warningly at where his hand rested, just a little too possessively and potentially betrayingly on her arm. 'Body language, Luc,' she reminded him under her breath. 'People are watching us.'

'Mmm...what do you mean, just as well I didn't?' Luc demanded, ignoring the second part of her comment.

'I never actually got as far as the cloakroom,' Belle informed him as they were caught up in the throng of people moving excitedly towards the exit so that they could watch the bride and groom leave.

'Why, what happened?' Luc asked her anxiously.

'My mobile started to ring,' Belle answered him, 'and once I realised who was calling I decided that it might be an idea to make sure I took the call in private. So I went out to the car.'

'In private?' Luc started to frown.

'Look over there at Luc and Belle,' Luc's mother sighed disappointedly at her husband as she caught sight of her son's frowning face.

'Just when I thought that the pair of them seemed to be getting on so well. I suppose I should have known it was too good to be true. And to think I'd actually begun to hope...' She shook her head ruefully. 'They always seemed so right for one another, and I can't help wishing...'

'Leave them to lead their own lives,' her husband advised her gently.

'In private,' Luc repeated with concern.

'Mmm...' Belle responded dreamily.

Belle's face was slightly flushed and Luc could almost feel the excitement bubbling up inside her. Her eyes, when he looked down into them, shone with barely concealed happiness. So much so that he could almost feel it radiating from her. She looked, Luc decided wryly, buoyed up with a secret—and with love.

'It must have been a very special call—and a very special caller.' Luc couldn't resist challenging her.

Belle's smile deepened, and so did her pretty pink colour.

'It was,' she admitted candidly.

'Belle, quick. She's leaving. Here...'

A handful of rose petals were pushed into Belle's hand by her mother, to shower onto the bride. Obediently, Belle turned her attention away from Luc and towards her niece and her new husband.

'Belle looks wonderful, doesn't she?' one of Belle's female cousins commented to another.

'Positively glowing...'

Belle, who had overheard their comment, waited until they were out of earshot before turning to Luc and remarking in a very, very soft whisper, 'Positively *blooming* might have been a more *appropriate* description—under the circumstances. Doubly so, in view of the fact…' She added mock coyly.

She stopped and waited for the penny to drop.

'My call was from the doctor's surgery,' she added helpfully, her own face breaking into a wide grin of excited happiness as she saw the enlightenment dawn in Luc's eyes.

'It's quite definitely twins,' she told him breathlessly.

'Twins… Two babies…' Luc gazed at her in adoring awe.

'Yes, twins does mean two babies,' Belle agreed teasingly, tongue in cheek.

She had had her suspicions for a while that she might be pregnant—she had even gone out and bought herself a home pregnancy test. But Luc had been away at the time, and in the end, she had wanted him to be there to share the moment with her. After all, he had been there—very much there— when their baby had been conceived, and they had agreed that this time round they were going to share their lives as true partners, true lovers.

Luc had been with her when she had first been told that she might be carrying twins, and today's phone call was the formal confirmation of the news they had already unofficially been given.

'Luc—Luc, stop it,' Belle protested as Luc suddenly wrapped her in his arms and gazed deeply into her eyes before starting to kiss her.

'Luc, people are watching us,' Belle protested

huskily beneath his mouth. 'Luc… Luc… Mmm… Mmm…'

'Let them watch,' Luc whispered back hoarsely.

Around them Belle could hear the astonished whispers of the other guests as they turned away from the departing bridal car to stare at Belle and Luc.

'I think we'd better tell them, don't you?' Luc whispered lovingly. 'Otherwise, if we don't…'

His hand covered her still flat stomach protectively, and even though she knew technically it was impossible as yet Belle could have sworn the two beings they had created with their love were kicking their assent to their father's suggestion.

'Well, they're going to have to know some time,' Belle agreed philosophically as she glanced down at her body. 'But a lot of them might not approve,' she warned him. 'After all, it's not exactly conventional.'

'We have the right to live our lives the way we want to live them, unconventional or not,' Luc argued softly.

And then, still holding her in the protective circle of his arm, he cleared his throat and began, 'Ladies and gentlemen, family and friends. Belle and I have an announcement to make.'

As he looked down at her, Belle looked back up at him, all the love she felt for him showing clearly in her eyes. A shaft of light touched the gold of the new wedding ring she had just removed from her purse and slipped onto her wedding finger—they had had it made from the gold of her old ring and

Luc's, a symbolic fusing of the old to create new in a bond that could never be broken.

Her sister saw it first, pre-empting Luc's announcement by screaming excitedly,

'Belle, you're married—you and Luc have re-married! Oh, how could you, without saying anything. Oh, Belle...Luc... Oh, this is so wonderful...'

'Wonderful,' Luc echoed as he raised Belle's hand to his mouth and gently kissed her fingers.

Through the excited hubbub that followed, Belle could hear her great-aunt Alice saying quite clearly to her mother, 'There you are, Mary, I knew I was right. They *are* married...'

As their relatives pressed happily around them, Belle could feel the joy bubbling up inside her.

Oh yes, they were married—had remarried. In a small, perfect, private ceremony on the island on the lake at Cheringham House, two weeks ago.

She had wanted to keep it a secret for just a little longer but... She patted her stomach tenderly.

Some events had a way of precipitating their own celebrations.

Above the heads of their excited audience Luc mouthed softly to her, I love you—and them.

Blissfully Belle returned his smile. One day—not this time, perhaps, but one day—they would have a little girl, and when they did, when they did, she rather thought they might call her Alice.

The Man She'll Marry

by

Carole Mortimer

CHAPTER ONE

'IS YOUR mother at home?'

Merry stared at the man who stood on the doorstep. She knew she was being rude; her 'mother' had taught her all the necessary social niceties. But, looking the way this man did, he had to be used to women staring at him. Dani would have described him as 'drop-dead gorgeous', and for the first time Merry understood exactly what she meant by that phrase; this man had to set female hearts pounding, pulses racing, wherever he went!

'Is Dani anything like you?'

The second question was fired at her before she'd even had chance to formulate an answer to the first one. It had been a long day, and she had only got in a short time ago, though long enough to have quickly changed into an old pair of black denims Dani had outgrown some years before, and a sloppy green jumper that hung loosely down to mid-thigh. Not exactly the height of fashion, but she was comfortable.

At least she had been, until faced with the elegance of her visitor. This man, well over six feet in height, with his 'drop-dead gorgeous' good looks—slightly overlong blond hair, a face that looked hewn from granite, eyes a deep blue, nose long and arrogant, mouth sensual above a squarely challenging jaw—wore his own designer-label clothes with a complete disregard for those labels, or for how well his blue jacket and pale blue shirt emphasised the width of his shoulders and the narrowness of his waist, his blue jeans simply adding to his rugged handsomeness. Dani's cast-offs, which were slightly too big at that, did not do the same for her own appearance!

He frowned at her now, although the laughter lines beside his eyes and mouth said he wasn't always this serious. '*Is* your mother at home?' he persisted.

'No,' she answered him honestly, intrigued in spite of herself. Oh, not by his looks; good looks alone had never impressed her. Well, only the once. And she had learnt bitterly from the experience. No, what intrigued her about this particular man was that he obviously knew of Dani but he had no idea what Dani actually looked like…!

Because Dani was nothing like Merry. Her own long hair was dark, almost black, whereas Dani's was a riot of blonde curls, and Dani's eyes were brown, whereas her own were green, and Dani, at eighteen, was much taller than her own five foot nothing. So who was this man? He knew *of* Dani, but nothing else about her—except her address…

He gave an impatient sigh. 'I don't suppose your sister is here, either? No.' He answered his own question. 'David said they were going to some coffee shop or other this evening. Damn,' he muttered, looking thoughtful. 'I don't suppose I could come in and wait, could I?' His imperious tone of voice totally belied the request that his words should have been.

A man used to getting his own way, Merry surmised ruefully. Probably in his late thirties, and with no ring on his left hand to say whether or not he was married. The fact that he wasn't wearing a ring said he would do as he damn well pleased, not that he wasn't actually *married*. Everything about this man quietly cried self-assurance and determination.

'No, I don't suppose you could,' she answered dryly.

Blond brows rose over those deep blue eyes, his mouth quirking wryly. 'Well, at least one of the family seems to have some sense!' he allowed.

She remembered again that it had been a long day and she had only been home from work for a short time; what she really wanted right now was to sit down with a glass of cooled white wine and simply unwind before thinking about preparing dinner. Her unexpected guest did not fit in with those plans at all. Besides, exactly what did he want to come in and wait *for*?

'One of the family?' she echoed smoothly, the mildness of her tone totally masking her impatience.

He nodded. 'You and Dani. You are obviously the elder—'

'Obviously,' she acknowledged crisply. Why state the *obvious*?

He gave her a sharp look, visibly making an effort to relax. 'I didn't mean to sound insulting, Miss Baker—'

'You may not have meant to, Mr...?' She paused

pointedly; he knew her name while she had absolutely no idea what his might be.

'Kingston,' he supplied. 'Zack Kingston.'

Merry frowned. Kingston? The name *did* sound familiar. Dani had mentioned someone at university by that name. David Kingston... 'David would be your son—'

'Nephew,' Zack Kingston corrected. 'Dani has obviously talked to you about him!'

Merry didn't like the accusation in his tone. Any more than she liked standing on the doorstep having this conversation with him. 'Mr Kingston, I was just about to have a glass of wine. Would you like to join me?' Green eyes steadily met blue.

How much 'sense' did he think she had now? The trouble with Mr Zack Kingston was that he formed snap judgements, and had taken one look at her and decided she was small and defenceless. It was only one of several wrong assumptions he had made!

That direct blue gaze was reassessing now, moving slowly from her bare feet, over the faded black denims, the too-large jumper, to the wild cascade of her long dark hair, the small gamine face dominated by challenging eyes.

To Merry's amusement, she could see he was none the wiser for his review of her. She obviously didn't look to him what she actually was. There was something to be said for a man-free—and therefore problem-free—life, after all!

'Make your mind up, Mr Kingston,' she advised mockingly. 'I don't intend standing here all evening waiting for your answer!'

Anger flared briefly in his deep blue eyes before

he quickly brought it under control. Here was a man used to calling the shots, Merry guessed again, not the other way around. Well, this was her home, and her time, and if he wanted to continue this conversation he could do it inside, where she could relax. She had absolutely no idea what he was doing here, what it had to do with Dani—if anything—and she had no intention of discussing it any further standing on the doorstep!

'You'll be quite safe, Mr Kingston,' she added derisively. 'I make it a rule never to attack defenceless men on—what is it today?—on a Tuesday evening,' she teased as she turned and walked back inside the house, sure he would follow her; he had come here this evening with something to say, and unless she was mistaken he hadn't said it yet!

'I can assure you, Miss Baker, I am far from defenceless!'

She was right; he *had* followed her! And as she looked up from pouring two glasses of wine she tried hard not to notice how his large frame dominated the bright but compact kitchen. 'You are?' she returned as she handed him his glass.

'I are— I mean— Oh, hell.' He scowled. 'Tell me, Miss Baker—'

'Merry,' she put in lightly, sitting up on one of the bar stools. 'Short for Meredith,' she tacked on, to save him the bother of asking; he was the sort of man who would want to know!

He nodded. 'Tell me, Merry,' he murmured softly as he sat on the second bar stool, his bent knee only inches away from her own. 'What happens to "defenceless men" on the other evenings of the week?'

Different approach. Anger hadn't worked, so now he was going to try cajoling, revealing some of that humour she had guessed at when she first saw him.

Merry quirked dark brows at him over the top of her wine glass. 'Why don't you come back tomorrow and find out?' she replied.

For a moment he looked perplexed. And then he smiled, and laughed.

Whew! Merry continued sipping her wine, mainly as a way of hiding the way her breath had caught in her throat. 'Drop-dead gorgeous'! That laugh only made him more so. A young Robert Redford, she decided admiringly.

He sobered, shaking his head as he still smiled. 'If Dani is anything like you, then I think I understand David's dilemma,' he said.

'David has a dilemma?' she prompted softly.

The laughter had all gone now; Zack Kingston's expression one of grim disapproval. '*I* consider it a dilemma, but I doubt that he does!'

Merry didn't understand how his nephew's dilemma could have anything to do with Dani. Dani had begun her studies at university at the end of September, and, being gregarious by nature, she had quickly made friends. David Kingston was only one of several Dani had mentioned during the last couple of months. Merry certainly couldn't think of any reason for the boy's uncle to come here in search of Dani...

'When do you expect your mother home?' Zack Kingston continued restlessly, putting down his glass of barely touched white wine.

Which wasn't altogether fair on the wine. Merry

didn't consider herself a connoisseur by any means, but her taste was discerning, and the wine was a delicious Chablis, perfectly chilled.

'I don't,' she told him consideringly. 'David's dilemma has something to do with Dani?' An uneasy fluttering sensation was beginning in the pit of her stomach.

Dani wasn't only gregarious, she was absolutely beautiful. And there was no bias involved in that observation; Dani had been bowling men off their feet since she was in her cradle!

'Tell me,' Merry said slowly, 'is David anything like you?'

'What the hell does that have to do——?' Zack Kingston broke off, shaking his head impatiently. 'David was the son of my older brother and his wife. Unfortunately they were both killed in a car accident ten years ago, which is when I took over his guardianship.'

Very commendable, considering the demands a child could make on you—even more so when he wasn't actually your own...

'That doesn't actually answer my question, Mr Kingston,' Merry persisted.

'I don't see what it has to do with anything——'

'It has a great deal to do with it,' she said tersely; a twenty-ish version of this man could be devastating to a girl like Dani. 'David is tall, blond, and gorgeous, right?'

Now he was the one to look mockingly at her. 'Like me?' he returned.

Merry glared at him. 'You're too old to be playing these sort of games, Mr Kingston——'

'The name is Zack—Merry,' he cut in. 'And I don't consider myself "too old" for anything!'

The chill in his tone would have frozen a lesser woman into silence, but Merry didn't consider herself a 'lesser' anything! And she never would!

'So David *is* like you?' she said irritably. Oh, Dani, sweet Dani, what have you done?

Zack shrugged. 'There's a certain similarity, yes. But—'

'It's enough,' Merry waved a dismissive hand. 'Dani told me she was meeting friends for coffee this evening. Am I to take it David is that friend?' Singular, not plural. But not exactly a lie, either. Not that she had thought for a moment that it would be; she and Dani had never lied to each other.

Those blue eyes were narrowed now. 'That's what he told me before he left this morning to attend classes, yes,' Zack agreed. 'Amongst other things,' he added. 'I called here earlier in the day in the hope I could talk to Dani's mother without—'

'I work, Mr Kingston,' Merry told him caustically. Unlike some people, obviously... The cut of his clothes, and that air of arrogance, spoke of wealth, and a nature that didn't suffer fools gladly. Well, she certainly didn't have the former, but she didn't suffer fools, either; and this man was taking an awful long time to get to his point!

He was staring at her now, seemingly speechless—not something that happened often, Merry was sure!

She had realised a few minutes ago that he assumed she was Dani's sister.

'I suggest we dispense with any misconceptions

you may have formed when you arrived, Mr Kingston,' she told him briskly. 'Dani doesn't *have* a sister, older or otherwise. In fact, Dani is an only child.' She met his eyes steadily.

Zack Kingston blinked, and then blinked again, his head tilted to one side as he reassessed the situation a second time. Finally he shook his head. 'You aren't old enough to be Dani's mother! Unless—' His gaze sharpened in dismay. 'Exactly how old is Dani?'

Merry was unabashed. 'Daniella—Dani—is eighteen.'

He looked relieved to hear that, but his puzzled vision returned to Merry once again, raking over her appearance once more, from the top of her head down to her bare toes, returning to her face—a face full of good humour, her green eyes clear and bright, her nose small and pert, her mouth wide and inclined to turn up at the corners, giving her a happy look even when she didn't feel much like smiling.

As she didn't now. This man, she had come to realise over the last few minutes, had come here to tell her something important about his nephew and her daughter. And in view of the way Dani had made her own way into life, Merry couldn't help the feelings of foreboding that were seething over her. She no longer found this man's mistake over her identity a cause for amusement, merely questioned the urgency of his need to talk to Dani's mother.

Zack drew in a controlling breath. 'Miss Baker— Er, Mrs—'

'*Miss* Baker,' Merry corrected stiltedly. What was that saying about 'the sins of the father'...? Did it also apply to 'the mistakes of the mother'? 'I've never been a Mrs Anything, Mr Kingston,' she informed him flatly, pointed chin raised defiantly.

He nodded abruptly. 'Well, Miss Baker, it appears you're about to have a wedding in the family now! My nephew David informed me this morning that he intends marrying your daughter!'

Merry swallowed hard, feeling the colour drain from her cheeks. Dani. Eighteen-year-old Dani. Beautiful Dani, who had her whole life before her. Dani, who had only been at university for two months. It couldn't be happening all over again!

Was the mistake of the mother being repeated by the daughter...?

CHAPTER TWO

'HERE, drink this,'

Merry looked up at Zack. 'This' turned out to be
what was left of the wine in his glass. There could
only be one reason—in the present circumstances!—
why Zack Kingston was encouraging her to drink it.

She pushed the glass away, glaring at him. 'I am
not in need of restorative alcohol, thank you,' she
told him frostily. 'Did you say you have been David's guardian for the last ten years?'

'Almost ten and a half, to be exact,' he confirmed,
frowning at the question.

Merry couldn't see what difference that six
months made! 'Oh, let's, by all means, be exact,'
she snapped caustically, looking him up and down,
once again noticing the expensive cut of his clothes,
his only jewellery a signet ring on the little finger
of his right hand. 'Are you married, Mr Kingston?'
she demanded in clipped tones.

His mouth twisted. 'Fortunately not.'

She had thought not; he didn't give the impression of a man in a hurry to get back to his home.
Or a wife. 'You do have some intelligence, then,'
she replied dismissively. 'In that case—'

'You consider it intelligent not to be married,
Miss—Merry?' he interrupted.

She looked at him pityingly. She could well un-understand his amazement at finding a woman who wasn't interested in marriage; considering the way he looked, his apparent wealth and his bachelor status, she could imagine he had met far too many women desperate to get married—to him!

'As I've already pointed out to you, marriage is an unknown quantity to me personally.' She shrugged. 'And it seems to me, from the amount of separation and divorce, that marriage has become an overrated state to be in!'

'You—'

'However, that does not mean I advocate single motherhood, either,' she continued firmly. 'I know from experience how hard that can be. For the mother left on her own to bring up the child, not the father,' she added heatedly. 'He usually walks away without any responsibilities!'

That deep blue gaze watched her consideringly. 'Is that what happened to you?'

She bristled defensively. 'We weren't talking about me!' Merry snapped back.

Zack shook his head dazedly. 'Then I would like to know who we are talking about?'

'Dani, of course!' Despite her refusal of his wine a few minutes ago, she now took a grateful sip from her own glass. 'You are the boy's guardian. Didn't you teach him any of the facts of life?' She shook her head with angry disgust. 'Or are you one of those men who believe it's the woman's responsibility to take care of the precautions?' That seemed all too often to be the case nowadays; woman's de-

mand for equality, and therefore independence, had
rebounded on them in the case of sexual relationships!

'Dani suffers from a similar problem to me, in
that she is medically unable to take the pill,' she
told Zack coldly.

'I'll file that information away for future reference,' he said, sounding amused.

Merry could feel the heat in her cheeks. This man
was making fun of her! 'I'm glad you find this situation funny, Mr Kingston—'

'"Funny" is far from the right word to describe
how I feel about what's happened,' he bit out, suddenly looking at her with an arctic chill in his eyes.
'You are obviously under some misapprehension
concerning Dani and David's relationship. Contrary
to the conclusion you seem to have jumped to, your
daughter is not pregnant!'

Merry stared at him uncomprehending. Not...?
When Zack Kingston informed her of his nephew's
determination to marry Dani, it had seemed to her
there could be only one reason for such impetuosity.
Distressing as that conclusion might have been. But
he was saying Dani *wasn't* pregnant!

'I don't understand.' She shook her head.

'I *didn't*,' he rasped. 'But, having now met you,
I'm beginning to!'

Merry looked at him blankly. What was that supposed to mean? What could she possibly have to do
with his nephew's announcement that he intended
marrying Dani; she had never even met the young
man!

'Perhaps you would care to explain that remark?' she invited coolly, green eyes sparkling.

He gave an abrupt laugh. 'I most certainly would,' he rasped. 'You obviously have an attitude towards pre-marital sex—'

'I have an attitude towards marriage too!' she jumped in. How dared this man come into her home and make snap judgements about her? He didn't even know her! He was an arrogant swine, and if he thought she was going to let her daughter have anything to do with a relative of his, then he was sadly—

'We'll get to that in a minute,' he dismissed, with that arrogance she had just mentally attributed to him. 'I was about to say that, in the circumstances, your attitude towards pre-marital relationships is perfectly understandable.'

'Exactly what "circumstances" would you be referring to, Mr Kingston?' Merry prompted fiercely, raising herself to her full height of five feet and half an inch—and making absolutely no impression on him, judging by the way he looked down his arrogant nose at her!

As she had expected, he looked unperturbed. 'Obviously the circumstances of Dani's birth—'

'Which you know absolutely nothing about!' she returned furiously. He raised his blond brows questioningly. Well, he could question all he liked; it was none of his business what those 'circumstances' might have been! Besides, he seemed to have already drawn his own conclusions.

The silence stretched between them, as green eyes

warred with blue. But Merry had no intention of being the one to back down.

'Which I know absolutely nothing about,' Zack was finally the one to slowly admit. 'But I believe it has everything to do with Dani's own feelings towards relationships.'

'You already said that,' Merry retorted.

His mouth tightened. 'Having now thought about this, it's my belief—though I won't be able to confirm this until I've spoken to David again—that he and Dani are in love, and that, like all young people in love, they wish to consummate their physical attraction towards each other, but that Dani would rather wait until after they are married.'

'I can't see anything wrong with that,' Merry scorned.

'There is if their only solution to the problem is for them to marry immediately!' Zack returned exasperatedly.

Dani had watched Merry's struggles over the years to cope with working and being a mother, and she knew exactly how difficult it had been for Merry to acquire a career at all when she had become pregnant during her first term at university. *Had* that coloured Dani's own views on marriage and lovemaking? If it had, was that really such a bad thing? Dani was so young still, not much more than a child, really, not old enough for the responsibility of either marriage or a family.

Thinking of Dani dissipated Merry's anger and distress, cleared the initial panic from her mind. She and Dani were close, and she didn't believe, now that she could think straight, that Dani would agree to marry someone and then not tell her own mother about it. Admittedly, Dani seemed to have kept the intensity of this particular relationship with David Kingston to herself, not seeming to have mentioned him any more than the other new friends she had made in the last couple of months. But a marriage proposal, and its acceptance, was something else entirely...

Merry looked up at Zack Kingston with a new confidence. 'I don't believe they *have* decided to marry, immediately or otherwise,' she told him calmly. 'I think you may have been a little premature in coming here today, Mr Kingston—'

'For God's sake call me Zack!' he exploded. 'And no matter what you may think, Merry, I did not imagine David's announcement to me this morning—it totally destroyed my appetite for breakfast!'

Merry felt her mouth twitching with humour, had to bite her lip to stop herself from smiling. She could picture Zack now, seated at the end of a long dining table, newspaper spread out in front of him, while some meticulous, silent servant served him bacon and eggs—the latter would be scrambled, of course, no messy egg-yolks for this man to deal with! And then, just as he was about to take his first mouthful of the mouthwatering food, David dropping his bombshell!

'I trust you managed to eat lunch, Zack?' she said soothingly. 'It really isn't good for the blood sugar for you to go without food for too long. It impairs your judgement, and—'

'My judgement is not impaired, Merry,' he bit out. 'David told me—'

'I'm not disputing what he told you,' she assured him evenly. 'I'm merely questioning the validity of the news that *Dani* intends marrying *him*. I must admit I was thrown for a few minutes after your initial announcement, but I've had time to collect my thoughts now. I know Dani, the two of us are friends, as well as mother and daughter, and if she were serious about your nephew then I believe she would have told me about him.' Merry's confidence increased even as she spoke the words. She *did* know Dani, and what this man was suggesting didn't sound at all like her daughter. 'I don't disbelieve that David told you how he felt towards Dani—'

'Thank you for that, at least!' Zack snapped with sarcastic impatience.

She couldn't exactly blame him for feeling this way; he had obviously had a tough day since David's intentions had destroyed his breakfast. They had certainly dispelled her own earlier tiredness too!

'I don't mean to sound patronising, Zack,' she assured him. She might not have meant to, but in retrospect that was exactly what she had sounded! 'I'm just doubtful of Dani's part in all of this.' She absently poured them both another glassful of wine, wordlessly handing his over. 'Dani and I have never had secrets. There's never been any reason for us to,' she revealed, thinking of her own years without romantic involvement.

When Dani had been very young there just hadn't been the time, between studying and caring for a young child, and there had only been the occasional date in the years following. Most men of a similar age to herself were either already married, running away from an unhappy relationship, or had no interest in a woman with a young child. None of them had appealed to Merry either. In fact, there had been no relationships that she couldn't happily talk to Dani about because there had been none that were serious!

'If Dani were in love,' she told Zack assuredly, 'then I believe she would have told me about it. And about him!'

'I—' Zack broke off as the sound of the front door opening and closing could clearly be heard.

'That will be Dani now,' Merry warned him softly, putting a lightly restraining hand on his arm. 'Let me handle this, please,' she advised gently as she heard Dani walking down the hallway.

'Mum, I'm home—' Dani broke off her cheerful greeting as she entered the kitchen and saw that her mother wasn't alone, her glance resting interestedly on the man who stood there.

Merry looked at her daughter with pride; she would never cease to be amazed that this gloriously beautiful creature was her own daughter. Almost six feet in height, Dani towered over her. Her hair was a long riot of honey-blonde curls that reached down the length of her spine, and her face as beautiful as any model's, with eyes of deep honey-brown.

Merry glanced sideways at Zack Kingston to see what his reaction was to this vision of loveliness that was her daughter. He looked stunned! But then so did every other man who looked at Dani. Including Zack's nephew, it seemed...

But, seeing Dani now, Merry was even more assured that her surmise concerning that situation was correct; Dani looked as carefree and open as she always did, and if she were hiding something as serious as a secret engagement then she wouldn't have done. Dani had never been any good at keeping secrets!

'Hello, darling.' Merry moved to hug her daughter. 'Had a good day?'

'Pretty good,' Dani responded vaguely, obviously fascinated by the man standing watching them from across the room—which wasn't surprising, considering what conclusion she must have come to concerning Zack's presence here; it was over a year since Merry's last date, and she certainly hadn't brought him home!

'This is Zack,' Merry introduced. 'He just called in for a chat,' she added meaningfully—for his benefit!

'Zack,' Dani greeted, politely shaking the hand he offered before turning to her mother. 'I'll just go and freshen up, and then I'll help you with dinner. Will you be eating with us, Zack?' she added mischievously, obviously intrigued by this male friend of her mother's who had just dropped by for 'a chat'.

Zack looked briefly at Merry. 'Er—no,' he answered huskily. 'As your mother said, I only called in briefly.'

'Oh, well.' Dani shrugged lightly. 'Perhaps I'll see you again some time.' She left the kitchen, her movements unconsciously graceful, taking her boundless energy and effervescence with her, her footsteps soft on the stairs.

Merry gave Zack another glance from beneath

lowered lashes. If he had looked stunned before, he now looked speechless!

He swallowed hard.

'She takes after her father,' Merry told him.

'Tall, blond, and gorgeous,' he acknowledged heavily.

Jeff had been all of those things. He had also been a lot of other things Dani wasn't...

'Yes,' Merry confirmed quickly. 'But the important thing is that Dani doesn't look to me like a young girl in the emotional throes of a secret love affair.'

'Or to me either,' Zack rejoined, obviously deeply annoyed now at the embarrassing situation he found himself in.

Which wasn't surprising, really. Zack Kingston gave every impression of being totally self-assured, in control of any situation he should happen to find himself in; Merry could only imagine the inner squirming he was going through at this moment!

'I think I'll take your advice and talk to David again,' he said grimly, putting down his empty wine glass. 'One of us has obviously got his wires crossed.'

As it wasn't Merry or Dani who were at fault, then the blame had to be on his side. Merry felt almost sorry for him. Almost... Except he had put her through some of the most traumatic moments of her life such a short time ago!

CHAPTER THREE

'YOU really should take more care, Merry,' drawled a familiar voice. 'I could have walked off with your handbag just now,' Zack pointed out.

Him again!

And she could see what he meant; her handbag was sitting on the bonnet of the car while she loaded her shopping into the boot.

She straightened. 'I doubt it, Zack,' she told him dryly. 'Mr Patel is a good friend of mine.' She nodded in the direction of the convenience store where she had just done her shopping; the sunny-faced proprietor was undoubtedly watching their exchange through the window. 'And if he failed to stop you, there's five pounds of potatoes in this bag.' She held up a plastic carrier before putting it into the boot with the rest of her bags. 'I would simply have hit you around the head with it!'

Zack's mouth twisted. 'And asked questions later!'

Merry nodded. 'When you regained consciousness, yes.'

He looked at her for several seconds, and then he chuckled, seemingly more relaxed today. 'You would, too!'

'Of course I would; I have all my money in there.'

She slammed the boot shut, taking her handbag from his unresisting fingers and placing it inside the car on the passenger seat. 'Wonderful as it is to see you again, Zack,' she said with no sincerity at all, as he made no effort to move away from the driver's door to allow her to get into her car, 'I do have to get on.' She looked up at him challengingly.

To her dismay, he looked just as gorgeous today as he had yesterday, the blue jumper that he wore so casually a perfect match in colour for those 'come-to-bed' eyes of his and he was slim and powerful in black denims.

After he had left her house the previous evening she had convinced herself that he couldn't possibly be as heart-stoppingly handsome as she had thought he was, but, looking at him now, in the rapidly fading daylight, she knew that he was even more so. In fact, he shouldn't be allowed out, was likely to cause traffic accidents. All to women, of course. Because instead of looking at the road they would be unable to take their eyes off Zack Kingston!

She had lain awake in her bed last night thinking about him. And then she'd been furious with herself. To lose sleep at all was bad enough, but to lose it over a man she hardly knew was unforgivable!

'I was just driving over to see you when I saw you come out of the shop,' Zack said, still leaning against the side of her car.

Merry stiffened. 'Why were you coming to see me?' she demanded warily.

'It seems I owe you an apology—'

'Accepted,' she said quickly, knowing exactly what he was apologising for. Casual conversation with Dani over dinner the evening before had assured her that Zack Kingston had definitely made a mistake where Dani and David were concerned.

David Kingston had only come into the conversation briefly, but it had been enough to tell Merry that her daughter had no more interest in him than she did in any of her other new friends at university. Dani certainly didn't know David well enough to realise he had *had* an Uncle Zack, let alone that she was expected to marry into his family!

'If I could just get into my car?' Merry asked pointedly; she was going to physically push him out of the way if he didn't move soon!

Zack gave her a quizzical look. 'Are you usually this rude?'

'With men that accost me in car parks? Yes!'

'So it was true, what you said about the other days of the week!'

She knew exactly what he was referring to. 'You aren't defenceless, Zack—on any day of the week!'

'True,' he responded. 'I would, however, like to make my apology properly—'

'The ground is too wet for you to get down on your knees,' she broke in disparagingly; it had been raining most of the day, adding to the misery of the cold November weather.

He shook his head, his eyes glowing with laughter. 'I had dinner more in mind than grovelling in front of you on my knees!'

Dinner? With this man? He had to be joking! She might as well stand in front of a double-decker bus and simply let it run her down. That was how dangerous she knew this man to be! And she had no intention of standing in front of that bus—or having dinner with Zack Kingston!

'For one thing, Zack,' she sighed, 'I have already accepted your apology—'

'I haven't made it yet,' he put in softly.

'For another—' she glared at him for the interruption '—I have just been into the shop and purchased the makings of dinner for Dani and myself.'

'That's fine,' he said. 'Dani wasn't included in the invitation anyway.'

'And for yet another,' she added with firm determination, 'I have no wish to go out to dinner with you!'

He folded his arms in front of his chest, leaning back against the door she wanted to open so she could get inside the car. 'Tell me,' he prompted lightly, 'have there been many men in your life since Dani's father?'

The question might have been casually put, but the audacity of it made Merry gasp. What on earth did it have to do with him? 'Mind your own damned business!' she responded indignantly.

'Hmm, I thought not,' he answered consideringly. 'Well, I'm thirty-nine years of age, and have never been engaged or married. Although I have no aversion to either state, I just didn't meet the right woman. I own a publishing house, have a home here in London and a villa in the south of France. I like children and dogs, and not necessarily in that order,' he added with a smile. 'Cats tend to make me sneeze, but if you happen to already have a cat, I'm sure I could learn to live with the sneezing. I—'

'Why are you telling me all these things?' Merry

finally managed to break in. This man had been an irritation in her life since—was it only yesterday they had met for the first time? It seemed like much longer! Now he wasn't just an irritation to her; he was fast becoming a nuisance!

He shrugged. 'Character reference. I realise all of this is usually covered in the first date, but as you refuse to even *have* that initial ceremony, I thought I should tell you a little about myself.'

'You missed out the bad points,' she taunted. First date, indeed!

He looked sceptical. 'I didn't know I had any,' he mocked.

Her eyes flashed deeply green. 'That arrogance is just one of them! You're also opinionated, judgemental, and—and you're so tall I get a crick in my neck just looking up at you!' she concluded irritably—and then felt irritated with herself. He was too tall…! What on earth was she talking—babbling—about?

It didn't help that Zack's grin widened at her remark. 'If we were seated at a dinner table that wouldn't happen,' he pointed out. 'It also wouldn't apply if we were lying—'

'You're so damned presumptuous!' she cut in huskily, her face fiery red. God, he had her blushing like a schoolgirl! But, considering she had met this man only about twenty-four hours ago, he was being damned familiar!

'On a beach somewhere warm,' he finished smoothly, blue eyes gleaming with laughter—at her expense. 'Don't you find the English winters cold and damp?' he continued, both of them knowing exactly what she had thought he was going to say.

'I love the cold and the damp of England.' She suppressed the shiver that just talking about it gave her. 'I can imagine nothing worse than spending Christmas on a hot beach somewhere.' She shook her head. 'Now, if you don't mind, my peas are defrosting and my chicken needs cooking!'

''I love roast chicken,' Zack told her hopefully.

'I'm deep-frying it.' She had just decided—stubbornly.

He shrugged. 'I can live with that.'

Merry stared at him exasperatedly. She didn't want to invite him to dinner. But as she looked up into his face, the arrogant set of his jaw, the unrelenting steel of his gaze, she had a feeling it wasn't going to be her decision.

Which was ridiculous. She was thirty-seven years old, totally independent; she didn't have to do anything she didn't want to do. And spending any more time in this man's company was not only stupid, it could be downright dangerous!

'Okay, but you're peeling the potatoes,' she heard herself say—her mouth functioning in total opposition to her brain—and then she found herself wondering if he knew *how* to peel potatoes. After all, a man who owned a publishing company, a house in London, *and* a villa in France, was also sure to have that army of servants, like the one she had envisaged serving him breakfast yesterday morning. The breakfast he hadn't been able to eat. Obviously there was nothing wrong with his appetite today! 'On sec-

ond thoughts, you can lay the table,' she decided—
if she had really decided anything at all...!

She had *decided* yesterday that she didn't ever
want to talk to this man again. And yet now she
appeared to be doing just that...

She also had no interest in having dinner with
him, either. And yet now it appeared she was going
to... Even if it would be in her own home, and he
was going to help her cook it!

Which was precisely what they were doing an
hour later, when Dani came into the house. This
time her daughter didn't just look surprised to see a
man in their kitchen—the same man as yesterday
evening!—she looked pleased too!

'Hi, Zack,' she greeted familiarly, bending to kiss
Merry lightly on the cheek before helping herself to
an apple from the fruit bowl, biting into it hungrily
as she sat down on one of the kitchen stools.

'You'll ruin your appetite for dinner,' Merry
chided indulgently; she knew from experience that
nothing dampened her daughter's love of food, and
yet she maintained a model-slim body. Dani could
probably eat six apples and manage to eat a full meal
afterwards!

Her daughter grinned dismissively. 'This is just
to tide me over until my pizza later.'

Pizza? But Dani *had* mentioned something this
morning about going out with some friends for a
pizza this evening...

Merry had forgotten the conversation during the
rush of the day, but it came flooding back to her
now. And Zack Kingston had invited himself to dinner. A dinner, it now appeared, they were going to

enjoy alone. Enjoy…? It was the last word she should have used to describe the next few hours she was going to have to spend in his company!

'I believe you know my nephew,' Zack put in conversationally, looking enquiringly at Dani. 'David. David Kingston,' he explained at Dani's blank look.

Dani's eyes widened. 'You're David's uncle?' she looked surprised—but nothing more than that, Merry noted with satisfaction. 'I would never have guessed.' Dani shook her head, grinning widely now. 'You look nothing alike, do you?'

Merry turned accusingly to Zack. When she had asked him yesterday he had told her that he and David had 'a certain similarity'. And she, she remembered now with an inward wince, had said, 'tall, blond, and gorgeous'!

'To look at, no,' Zack replied. 'But in temperament we're very similar,' he amended, with a mocking sideways glance at Merry.

Arrogant, opinionated, and judgemental! Thank goodness Dani *wasn't* heavily involved with the younger Kingston!

'How incredible!' Dani jumped lightly to the floor, almost as tall as Zack in her heeled boots. 'David's coming out for a pizza with us; I can't wait to tell him you're here having dinner with my mother!' She looked pleased at the thought.

'Dani!' Merry panicked at the thought of her daughter leaving her alone here with Zack.

'I'm only going upstairs to change, Mum,' Dani assured her lightly. 'I'll come back in and say goodbye before I leave.'

'I hope you all have a good time,' Zack put in agreeably, moving so that he stood beside Merry, his arm curving about her shoulders. 'And don't feel you have to hurry back,' he tacked on laughingly.

Merry looked up at him sharply, just in time to see him give Dani a conspiratorial wink. Really! The man had come here yesterday, breathing fire and accusations about her daughter, and now he was giving Dani the impression that the two of them, that he and she, were— There was no 'he and she'!

'Gotcha,' Dani shot back at him before Merry could say anything. 'I'll be down again in about ten minutes,' she warned teasingly, before leaving them alone in the kitchen.

Merry moved pointedly out of the curve of Zack's arm, turning to face him accusingly. 'Exactly what do you think you're doing?' she demanded, green eyes bright with annoyance. 'Dani now thinks— She now has the impression—' Merry could hardly speak!

'Would you rather Dani knows I came here on a wild-goose chase yesterday?' Zack asked. 'That she be made aware of the fact that David made a declaration concerning her of which she has no knowledge? I spoke to David last night,' he added at Merry's questioning look, 'and learnt that he's never so much as taken her out on her own, let alone kissed her or told her he's in love with her! What he was actually saying to me yesterday morning was that he's *seen* the girl he wants to marry, not that he has actually asked her and has been accepted!' he explained.

That was more or less the conclusion Merry had

come to—once she'd been able to think at all! And, no, she didn't want to humiliate David Kingston by telling Dani what had happened yesterday. That would only be embarrassing for everyone involved.

Besides, she had done things, made statements herself, at the same age, that hadn't always been tactful or well thought out...

'You told me that David looks like you!' she attacked, not willing to let this man off the hook quite that easily. After all, he was the one who had over-reacted...

'No, I didn't,' Zack denied easily. 'I said there was "a certain similarity". And I wasn't referring to the way we look. David is several inches shorter than me, with the dark colouring of his mother. But he's very like I was at his age, over-serious and hard-working—that was the reason I made the jump in assuming his relationship with Dani was an actual thing; David doesn't make light-hearted statements.' He looked rueful. 'He still hasn't. We talked a little about Dani last night, and although the relationship hasn't gone anywhere so far, I can assure you he does intend marrying her!'

'Dani is too young to marry anyone just yet,' Merry insisted stubbornly. 'No matter how serious and hard-working your nephew might be!'

Zack seemed unfazed. 'I would say that's for the two of them to sort out, in their own time. Hopefully, not for several more years yet.' His mouth quirked. 'That's definitely one aspect of mine and David's personalities that differs. Or maybe it's just that I'm older and so there doesn't seem to be so much time; David has immense patience, whereas

I—I don't have any patience at all. But then neither of us are children, are we, Merry?' he finished with satisfaction.

She gave him a startled look. *'We..?'*

He nodded. 'David may have taken one look at Dani and decided he wants to marry her, but yesterday I did the same thing where her mother was concerned. That's why, when you asked me, I counted it fortunate that I wasn't already married. You see, there *is* going to be a wedding in the family after all, Merry—ours!'

She had felt this way when she was a child, riding on the merry-go-round, slightly dizzy, slightly disorientated—and very definitely speechless!

CHAPTER FOUR

THE feeling didn't last very long—thank goodness!

'You didn't tell me that insanity ran rife in your family!' she burst out, moving a suitable distance away from him. As much as the confines of her kitchen would allow!

He and his nephew were prime candidates for treatment as far as she was concerned. Dipsticks. Fruit loops. One slice short of a loaf.

However it was put, Zack Kingston was definitely deranged!

He smiled at her now, that slow, lazy smile that only made him appear more handsome. What a pity he was also insane!

'It doesn't,' he answered her easily.

'Then it's just you and David who are afflicted,' she accepted. A day ago she had been quietly living her life, completely unaware of the existence of Zack and David Kingston. And she would like to go back to that unawareness!

Zack shook his head, perfectly relaxed as he leant back against one of the kitchen units, smiling unconcernedly, appearing completely unabashed by the fact that he had just announced his intention of marrying her.

'David and I both have an IQ of over one hundred and fifty,' he drawled mockingly.

'Which just goes to prove the point of that saying "there's a very fine line between genius and insanity"!' Merry cried. 'David appears to be pretty close, but you are obviously way over the edge!'

Zack chuckled softly. 'One of the things I like about you is your sense of humour.'

She shook her head pityingly. 'I wasn't joking.'

'I know that,' he sobered. 'But I wasn't joking either,' he told her seriously.

Completely off his trolley, Merry decided. Thank goodness Dani hadn't gone out yet; she might need some help getting Zack out of the house.

'Mr Kingston—Zack,' she amended soothingly as he raised his brows at the formality; no point in disturbing him unnecessarily! 'How many women have you invited to marry you this week?' she prompted conversationally, willing Dani to finish changing and come back down the stairs. She needed her assistance!

He met her gaze unblinkingly, although there was laughter in the depths of his clear blue eyes. 'I can say with all honesty—'

'Honesty is good,' Merry encouraged, still eyeing him warily.

He gave an inclination of his head. 'I think so too. Dishonesty engenders mistrust, and a relationship cannot be built on either of those things.' He straightened. 'As I told you yesterday, I am thirty-nine years old, and in all that time I have suggested marriage to only one woman. You,' he added, so that there could be no misunderstanding on her part.

Her... Why her? What had she done to deserve being singled out in this way? Or perhaps that was it; she had made no secret of her feelings towards men and marriage, and maybe Zack Kingston was one of those men who couldn't resist a challenge? Well, he was going to find her a lot more than a challenge!

'I'm sure it's a great honour, Zack,' she told him with heavy sarcasm. 'But my answer has to be no.'

His mouth twisted. 'I haven't asked you yet,' he reminded her.

No, he hadn't asked, but he had told! 'I'm advising you to save your breath,' she bit out impatiently.

'Oh, I don't intend asking you until I'm sure you'll say yes,' he assured her.

'Indeed? Has someone given you prior knowledge of hell freezing over?' she said pleasantly.

Zack chuckled again. 'See what I mean? Great sense of humour.'

'I wasn't joking,' she snapped. 'I'm sure you're a great marital catch, Zack.' If one overlooked the insanity! 'Passably good-looking.' Gorgeous! 'Rich.' The Jaguar XJS that he had driven while he followed her home was testament to that! 'It's just that I've reached the age of thirty-seven without marrying anyone—and I have no immediate plans to change my status!' Dani, where are you? she mentally pleaded with her absent daughter. 'And, in the circumstances, I don't think it would be a good idea for you to stay to dinner,' she finished reasoningly.

'That's a bit unfair—since I helped to cook it,' he protested lightly.

Peeling four potatoes, and two of them for himself, did not constitute helping her cook dinner as far as she was concerned! Although she accepted it was probably the first time Zack had ever peeled even *one* potato—judging by the amount of potato he had cut off with the peel, his hundred and fifty-something IQ obviously served him no useful purpose when it came to practicalities!

'Besides,' he went on persuasively, 'you need someone to help you eat all that food now that Dani is going out.'

Merry's mouth set. 'I don't wish to seem rude, Zack—'

'Of course you do,' he laughed. 'It's another part of your charm.'

Being rude was charming? This man certainly had a warped sense of what he found attractive in a woman. Or perhaps it was just that he was surrounded by yes-men—and women—most of the time...?

'Thank you,' she dismissed. 'I think I'm beginning to understand now why it is you've never married before; you only want to marry women who have no interest in you!' Although, his insanity aside, she didn't think there could be too many of those—besides herself!

He laughed once more, not at all perturbed by her insult. 'That's quite an interesting theory, Merry.' He moved to pour some of the wine from the half-bottle that had been left from the evening before, handing her one of the glasses. 'Completely untrue, of course. But interesting.' He sipped his wine thoughtfully. 'I would just like to repeat that I had never asked *any* woman to marry me before I met you.'

'Then why change the habit of a lifetime?' Merry prompted desperately, taking a thirsty gulp of her wine—a wine, moreover, that was supposed to be sipped and enjoyed, not thrown down the throat like its cheaper imitators. But this man, with his determination, was starting to grate on her nerves.

'You see,' he grinned. 'Life with you will never be boring!'

'I can be boring—if that's what it takes to get rid of you!' she assured him.

Zack folded his arms. 'I'm not going anywhere.' And, as if to prove his point further, he made himself comfortable on one of the kitchen stools.

'I'm thirty-seven—'

'You don't look it,' he assured her admiringly.

'A single mother—'

'We can have more children, if you would like them,' he confirmed softly.

Merry glared at him. He had deliberately misunderstood the statement. 'I spend my days working—'

'Wonderful,' he agreed.

She drew in a breath. 'My nights—'

'We'll get to your *nights* in a moment,' he butted in. 'I'm interested in what sort of work you do.'

'It's completely unnecessary for you to know what work I do—considering we are never going to meet again after tonight!' Merry glared at him.

Zack remained unruffled. 'Humour me,' he encouraged.

She had been humouring him for the last ten

minutes; in any other circumstances she would have got as far away from him as possible. But as it was her home he was the one who had to leave. Something he didn't seem inclined to do!

She turned off the heat beneath the potatoes, having no interest in eating them now; a proposal of marriage was sure to rob her of her appetite! 'I teach,' she told him abruptly.

'Subject?'

She sighed. 'Art,' she told him, tensing as she waited for his scorn.

She had heard all the criticism about teaching art, mostly that it was a waste of time—her own and her pupils'. She didn't happen to agree with those critics, felt there was so much more to individuals than their academic capabilities, that there was an artist of some sort inside everyone.

'I should have guessed,' he murmured softly. 'There's a certain style to the way you look and dress,' he explained at her frowning look.

Merry looked down at her long floral skirt and the skimpy black top she wore with it. 'Today's "style" is a charity shop,' she told him dryly. 'And yesterday's was post-Dani; I don't have a lot of spare cash to spend on stylish clothes for myself.' She gave a pointed look at his own expensively tailored clothes.

'I acknowledge the put-down, Merry,' he accepted. 'But I certainly wasn't being patronising—as you thought I was,' he guessed correctly. 'Some people have a style of their own, so much so that they look good in whatever they wear—you are one of those people.'

There wasn't a lot she could say to a remark like

that. Fashionable clothes had never been something she was too interested in—just as well, in the circumstances. But over the years she had developed a certain style she considered her own, one that suited the slenderness of her figure and the dark wildness of her long hair. What surprised her was that Zack Kingston had recognised it as such...

Now who was being patronising? Wasn't she giving in to a little reverse snobbery here? Which was totally unlike her. She liked her life the way it was, loved her job, being mother to Dani, and never minded that most people had more money than she did. Even if she had money herself, there was nothing about her life she would want to change. Well... Perhaps one thing. But that was only a dream of hers...

'Thank you,' she accepted huskily.

'Don't be too quick to thank me, Merry,' he replied, blue eyes alight with wicked humour. 'I've also spent a considerable amount of the last twenty-four hours imagining what you would look like *without* the clothes!'

She drew in a shaky breath, colour burning her cheeks as she stared at him wide-eyed. 'You—'

'I'm off now, Mum.' Dani bounced back into the room, lovelier than ever in a brown fitted top and brown jeans that hugged the perfection of her statuesque figure. 'Enjoy your evening.' She grinned at both of them.

'Are you sure you wouldn't like to join us for dinner before you go out?' Merry pressed. 'We— I've cooked plenty,' she amended, annoyed with herself for even verbally coupling herself with Zack

Kingston. For goodness' sake, he had been fantasising about her *naked*!

Dani looked puzzled. 'I thought I explained; we're all having pizza.' She gave a hurried glance at her watch. 'I really do have to go now, or I'll be late.'

'Dani?' Zack called to her as she was leaving the room. 'Have you ever been a bridesmaid?' She turned back to him questioningly.

'A bridesmaid?' she repeated. 'No, I—' Her eyes widened as she looked at the two of them, Zack so quietly self-assured, her mother now ashen-faced.

Merry had eyes for no one but Zack, her whole body tense with fury. 'You are taking this joke too damned far!' she bit out forcefully, hands clenched tightly at her sides.

Ordinarily a woman who abhorred violence, she was in danger of hitting him! He had walked into their lives—invaded them!—but he certainly wasn't staying!

'Go ahead and enjoy your evening, Dani.' She spoke as calmly as she could to her daughter, even managing to smile a little. 'Mr Kingston's idea of a joke seems to be vastly different from ours,' she added scornfully.

Dani glanced at him, and then she turned back to Merry—as if she very much doubted he would joke about something like that. 'Sure, Mum,' she said, taking her leave this time without any hindrance.

The silence she left behind her was so heavy with tension it could have been cut with a knife...!

CHAPTER FIVE

'YOU may have helped me prepare the dinner, Zack,' Merry told him flatly. 'But this last fifteen minutes in your company has completely robbed me of any desire to eat!' She turned off the oven—having decided to roast the chicken pieces, after all!

'Love,' he informed her unconcernedly. 'They tell me it does that to you,' he explained at her enquiring look.

Her brow cleared, her exasperation rising. 'Zack, I am not in love. With you or anyone else!' she pronounced firmly. 'I don't even know you. And what I do know I don't particularly like!'

'You've already said that,' he replied. 'For "arrogance" I think you should read self-assurance. For "opinionated" probably straightforward.' He began to tick off the list of her earlier accusations concerning his nature. '"Judgemental"? No—I don't think so. As for the being tall part, I could just as easily make the observation you're a little on the short side.' He looked at her, a smile playing around his lips.

As well it might. There was certainly nothing wrong with his memory! Even down to that last babbling comment she had made about his height...! Except that it *had* been complete babbling; his height, that air of self-assurance, all combined to make her feel small and feminine. She had battled so hard for years not to feel that way, not to need anyone, to rise and fall on her own merits. And, even if she said so herself, she hadn't done too bad a job of it.

But Zack Kingston, with his smooth self-confidence, made her feel vulnerable, while at the same time his admiration of her independent nature gave her a confidence in that vulnerability. Dangerous territory, indeed...

She couldn't actually be feeling attracted to this man! Could she...?

She glanced across at him, only to find he was staring right back at her. As he saw the confusion in her expression he stood up, moving slowly across the kitchen towards her.

He was going to kiss her, she decided in the split second before he gathered her into his arms and did exactly that!

Insane or not, Zack certainly knew how to kiss, his mouth insistent, and yet at the same time infinitely tender. And then his kiss deepened, passion flaring between them as Zack's arms tightened and his lips became more demanding on hers.

She responded. She would have been lying if she'd tried to claim that she didn't. Her arms up about his neck as she stood on tiptoe to meet him, the curves of her body somehow seeming to fit perfectly into his. Which was odd, given the difference in their heights...

'Mum, could I—? Oops!' gasped a surprised Dani.

Merry broke quickly away from the strength of Zack's arms, though he was reluctant to release her. She moved several feet away from him, turning to look at Dani as she stood wide-eyed in the doorway. Which wasn't surprising; Merry couldn't remember the last date she had been on, let alone when she had last been kissed. And her daughter certainly hadn't been a witness to it!

Merry took a deep breath, her cheeks fiery red. 'Yes, Dani?' Her voice sounded slightly huskier than usual, but at least she had managed to speak!

Flustered as she felt, she hadn't been sure she would be able to speak at all. She still trembled from the intensity of the passion that had risen so quickly between Zack and herself.

Dani looked slightly embarrassed at having interrupted so intimate a situation. 'I forgot earlier. We thought we might all go back to Jane's after our pizza and listen to music. I wondered if I could borrow some of your CDs?' She grimaced her regret at having burst in on them.

'Er—yes, of course you can.' Merry still felt flustered, while Zack, damn him, appeared completely unruffled. Appeared... Because a closer look showed her that his hands, which he was thrusting into his trouser pockets, were shaking a little. Not so unconcerned, after all. 'They're in the lounge,' she told Dani. 'Help yourself.'

'Thanks.' Dani looked relieved at being allowed a quick getaway. Although she paused at the door. 'I promise I won't be back again for hours,' she said mischievously.

'Tactful young lady,' Zack murmured once he

and Merry were alone again, the front door closing firmly behind Dani as she left—'for hours'! 'So you like music, too?' he continued, before Merry could make the sharp reply she wanted to. 'David plays music all the time when he's at home,' he explained at her questioning look. 'Consequently I find that my music tastes don't match those of my peers'. He shrugged. 'I suppose that's what happens when you have a teenager constantly about the house.' He certainly wasn't complaining about it, merely making an observation.

Merry hadn't quite looked at it in this way before, but, even though their circumstances were vastly different, Zack was, in effect, a single parent too...

'Not so different, after all, are we?' Zack drawled as he watched the candid emotions flickering across her face.

Her defences were certainly slipping where he was concerned—and it simply wouldn't do!

'Oh, but we are,' she dismissed scathingly. 'No doubt you were able to hire a nanny for David when he was younger—' She broke off as Zack shook his head.

'I felt David had already suffered enough heartache losing his parents at such a young age, and it didn't seem fair that I farmed the responsibility of him out to someone else. So during school terms I fitted my work in around his hours, and during the holidays I worked mainly from home.'

'The benefit of being your own boss?' Merry derided, not letting him off that easily.

'Possibly, Merry,' he accepted harshly. 'Although ten years ago Thorndyke Brooks was a struggling publishing house, and a lot of work was involved in making it viable again.'

Her eyes widened. 'It's Thorndyke Books that you own?'

Now one of the top publishing houses, ten years ago it had been on the brink of bankruptcy. Zack Kingston was the entrepreneur who had stepped in and turned the company around? Very successfully, if she remembered correctly. They had a dozen international top authors working for them now, and their non-fiction books were of a very high standard indeed—several Thorndyke textbooks were used at the school where Merry worked.

'You're *that* Kingston?' His business successes had been reported in the newspapers for years, but somehow she had always imagined—if she had thought of it at all!—that he would be older. Much older...

'It is. And I am,' Zack confirmed. 'And you're changing the subject, Merry,' he added with gentle reproof. 'I was endeavouring to point out the things we do have in common, not the things we don't.'

She knew what he had been doing—which was precisely the reason she had tried—and apparently not succeeded!—in putting him on the defensive for a change. She didn't want to have things in common with Zack; it was so much easier to believe their lives—and consequently the two of them!—were completely incompatible.

'You can't do that, Zack,' she denied, smiling wryly. 'The one doesn't outweigh the other.'

'It would be extremely boring if we were exactly the same, Merry,' he returned dryly. 'It's the differences that add the spark. For instance, I like not knowing what you are going to do or say next.'

She pulled a face. 'I'm going to say something I've already said several times this evening—dinner is off!'

His blue eyes glittered teasingly. 'It's a terrible waste of food, and you don't strike me as a woman who approves of waste,' he responded softly. 'Besides, it's my cook's night off, so you'll be condemning me to a takeaway if you make me leave now.'

'You could always join Dani and David for a pizza,' Merry suggested mockingly.

Zack grimaced. 'The pizza would be fine; it's all those over-intense students I'd find hard to stomach. I can't believe we were ever like that, can you?'

He was doing it again, and it wasn't going to work this time. 'I'm not sure I like being a stand-in for your cook!' She took the plates out of the warmer and began to dish up the food that was rapidly spoiling.

'If you could see Mrs Jenkins you would realise exactly how untrue that remark is!' He grinned, straining water from the peas without being asked. 'I'm quite self-sufficient, Merry,' he stated as she watched his efficient movements. 'I only employed a cook once David came to live with me. Bachelor fare isn't suitable for a growing child.'

She laughed, able to imagine what sort of food he had eaten when he was on his own. 'I'm sure David wouldn't have minded!'

'Maybe not,' Zack accepted. 'But I take my duties as his guardian rather seriously.'

Merry gave him a humorous glance. 'So I noticed yesterday,' she came back.

He grinned again that boyish, heart-stopping grin that was so hard to resist. 'I don't regret yesterday. Oh, I wish I hadn't walked in here with all guns firing and made such an idiot of myself,' he admitted. 'But at the same time, if I hadn't, then I wouldn't have met you.'

There was no answer to that, so Merry didn't make one. 'Would you like to eat here or in the dining room?' The food was served onto the plates now, and needed to be eaten before it got cold.

'Here will be just fine,' he assured her. 'I have a bottle of wine for us in the car. I'll just go and get it.'

A bottle of—? He had intended having dinner with her this evening no matter what!

'Close your mouth, Merry.' He bent and kissed her. 'Find me a corkscrew to open it with, would you?' he instructed, before striding outside to his car.

He couldn't just walk in here and take over! He couldn't— He already had...! She wasn't used to this, had been on her own too long to meekly accept—

Her outraged thoughts came to an abrupt halt as Zack returned to the kitchen and she saw the bottle of wine in his hand. It was exactly the same vintage and from the same region as the one she had given him last night—her favourite wine, a small luxury she allowed herself from time to time. She didn't believe for a moment that it was a coincidence—or indeed a shared taste—that had prompted Zack to choose it; he had clearly made a mental note of it the evening before, and deliberately brought a bottle for them to drink together this evening...

'It's quite chilled from being outside in the car,' Zack told her as he took the corkscrew from her unresisting fingers.

Merry was glad of his concentration on removing the cork from the bottle so that she had time to blink back the tears that were threatening to fall. It had been so long since anyone had cared enough to have noticed such a small detail as the wine she liked to drink. If anyone ever had! Oh, Dani was wonderful, and took a lot of care over birthday and Christmas presents, but Merry doubted that even her daughter had taken the trouble to note what wine she favoured.

But Zack had. And he had noticed her individual style of dressing too...

He was far too observant for comfort. Too much time spent in the company of someone so attentive and she might even start to—No! She was not going to fall in love with Zack Kingston. He wasn't right for her at all. He wasn't just attentive, he took over! He—

'To us.' Zack held out one of the glasses of wine to her, challenge in every muscle of his body as he waited for her to return the toast.

'To Christmas,' she returned dryly, refusing to return such an intimate toast. There wasn't an 'us', and there never would be!

'Just as good,' he nodded his satisfaction. 'Excuse the pun,' he went on, 'but I have the feeling it's going to be a very *Merry* Christmas now that I've met you!'

Merry was quite happy to excuse his pun, it was the quiet determination in his voice that bothered her!

CHAPTER SIX

'TALKING of Christmas—'

'You were; I wasn't,' Merry quipped. The two of them, having enjoyed their meal—and the wine!— were now seated in the sitting room in front of the roaring fire Zack had insisted he build for them in the grate. Merry's reluctance to have him light the fire hadn't stemmed from a need to be independent, but from the fact that she knew it was all too cosy and comfortable with the flames glowing!

Zack looked unconcerned by her interruption. 'I have a pre-Christmas cocktail party I have to attend tomorrow evening. I wondered if you would like to come with me?'

Merry just stared back at him. A cocktail party. Did she look like the type who went to *cocktail parties*?—where dozens of bored people, who usually didn't know each other very well, stood around with drinks in their hands, nibbling away at unrecognisable canapé that did absolutely nothing to satisfy one's hunger. She might have a tiny build, but she had a healthy appetite—as this evening's meal should have told him!—and the thought of spending hours at this man's side, trying to look decorous, did not appeal to her one little bit. Besides—

'I'll take your silence as acceptance—'

'I shouldn't if I were you,' Merry calmly stopped him. 'Cocktail parties aren't my scene.'

'If you're worried about being fed, I promise I'll take you out to dinner later in the evening,' Zack assured her dryly.

She gave him a glare, more because he *had* realised she appreciated her food than anything else. 'You're jumping two steps ahead, Zack, when I've already turned down the original request!'

'Oh, come on,' he cajoled. 'What harm can it do you to come along with me? You'll stop me being bored out of my mind!'

It couldn't do her any harm; she was more than capable of looking after herself! That wasn't the point of her refusal at all. She was an adult, and for the most part she could pick and choose what she did. Accompanying this man to a cocktail party was not high on her list of priorities.

But, a little voice inside her head reasoned, Zack *had* helped her unpack her shopping earlier, *had* helped her to cook dinner, *and* he'd produced a bottle of her favourite wine for them to drink with it. He—

None of those things changed the fact that he had also announced his intention of marrying her!'

In that case, she asked herself almost a day later, as she studied her reflection in the mirror, what on earth was she doing all dressed up as she waited for Zack to arrive before driving them both to the cocktail party?

Merry shook her head dazedly; the man was like a steamroller, knocking down any obstacles—including the word 'no'!—that got in his way.

She looked at her appearance critically. Not bad, she decided. Not bad at all. The black fitted knee-length pencil-slim dress was almost twenty years old, but it was back in fashion, and considering the amount of times she had found to wear it during those years—nil!—it was in pristine condition. Her figure had returned to its natural slenderness after she had given birth to Dani. Her hair she had left loose in dark curls down her spine, adding a little make-up to her normally peachy complexion and a peach gloss to her lips. Yes, she didn't look bad at all for a thirty-seven-year-old mother...!

She gave a rueful smile as she turned away from the mirror. She didn't look bad, but a thirty-seven-year-old woman, with an eighteen-year-old daughter, was *exactly* what she was—and the sooner Zack realised it the better!

But Dani's comment, when Merry walked down the stairs a few minutes later, did nothing to reassure her she would convince him of that this evening.

'You look gorgeous, Mum!' Dani announced admiringly. 'I don't think I've seen you in that dress before.'

Merry smiled. 'If you had, no doubt you would have borrowed it before now!' Dani was a lot taller than her, but both of them had size ten figures.

Dani touched the silkily soft material. 'It's beautiful, Mom. It must have cost—' She broke off as the doorbell rang.

'That will be Zack,' Merry said gratefully—she had never thought she would be relieved at his arrival, but on this occasion she most certainly was.

She did not want to get into a discussion with

Dani about her dress... Maybe she shouldn't have worn it, but quite honestly she just didn't have anything else suitable to wear. Cinderella in reverse. She did have something to wear to the ball—but that something had already provoked her daughter's curiosity...

Other than telling her she looked beautiful, Zack made no comment on the dress. But Merry somehow doubted its designer-label style had missed his eagle-eyed attention.

She shouldn't have worn it, did not want to pique Zack's interest in her any more than it already was piqued. But the temptation not to look like the poor relation had been too much for her. Vanity. Ridiculous, in the circumstances...

'David and Dani are going to the cinema together this evening,' Zack announced as he drove them to the party.

'I know,' she replied. 'And until a few days ago—' until Zack himself had come into their lives! '—Dani was barely aware of your nephew's existence.' Any more than she had been aware of Zack's! 'Obviously optimism runs in the family!'

Zack grinned unabashedly. 'I told you, David is a lot like me.'

And what David hadn't been able to achieve on his own—Dani noticing him as more than just one of the crowd!—his uncle had done for him. Dani was now intrigued by the Kingston family. David, she had informed Merry earlier, was a very intelligent young man. Dani had never been attracted to overtly good-looking young men, was more interested in the brain behind the looks. Remembering

Dani's father, and the way she herself had stupidly fallen for his golden good looks, it was a trait Merry had encouraged in her daughter. David Kingston, Dani had decided, had an 'intelligent' mind...

'I know, I know,' Zack said as he saw Merry's expression. 'I was mad as hell two days ago at the thought of David wanting to marry anyone. But, having now met Dani...' He paused. 'She's too much like you to be pushed into anything she doesn't want to do.'

'Remember that,' Merry returned quickly, trying to salvage at least some control over what was happening in her own life. This man was a bulldozer, and at the moment she didn't seem to be holding her ground at all. As evidenced by this evening! 'Exactly where is this party?' She changed the subject as she straightened her colourful shawl, its long length covering the dress totally.

'A hotel in the city,' Zack returned economically.

There was something to be said for being driven in the luxury of the XJS, the smell of doe-leather, the warmth of the interior.

The close proximity of Zack in the confines of the sports car...

He looked, and smelt, gorgeous, the black dinner suit and snowy white shirt doing nothing to hide the power of the body beneath, his hair newly washed and gleaming golden, his aftershave elusively male. No doubt heads would turn—female, of course!—when they reached the party.

Although she was unprepared for the absolute silence that greeted their entry into the crowded private room where the party was being held, or the spontaneous applause that quickly followed that silence.

Merry turned to look behind her, expecting to see someone famous entering behind them. But only Zack and herself stood in the doorway. And as they couldn't be clapping her...

She turned frowningly to Zack as the tiny band at the other end of the room began to play 'For He's a Jolly Good Fellow'. Exactly what sort of party was this? And why was Zack being welcomed in such a fashion?

An elegantly dressed woman in her fifties moved forward out of the crowd to kiss him warmly on the cheek. 'Wonderful party, Zack,' she congratulated throatily.

Merry knew this woman, recognised her instantly. It would be difficult not to; Diana Melbrook was the author of several number one bestselling books, her last having been turned into a television mini-series. The authoress had appeared on several chat shows in the weeks preceding its broadcast.

As Merry glanced around the room she saw several other well-known people: top authors, several actors, a number of television personalities too.

This wasn't just any old cocktail party Zack had brought her to, this was a Thorndyke Books cocktail party—and Zack, as the owner of the publishing house, was also the host!

What did that make her...?

CHAPTER SEVEN

'YOU'VE stopped smiling,' Zack murmured softly against her ear as the conversation began to flow around them once again and they were no longer the centre of attention.

Stopped smiling? That was the least of her worries! She felt frozen to the spot by what she had just realised, wasn't sure she was going to be able to move when the time came for them to mingle with the other guests.

She had imagined a large, impersonal party, a short time spent in inane conversation with complete strangers, and then the two of them could quietly leave. As the host of this party, Zack could hardly leave until the last guest had gone. Which could be in several hours' time!

She turned to him accusingly. 'You could have warned me!'

He spoke unconcernedly. 'If I had, you wouldn't have come.'

'Of course I wouldn't—' She broke off, breathing deeply to steady her nerves. 'What am I supposed to do now?' Her glittering green gaze told him of her tension.

'Enjoy yourself?'

Enjoy herself...? She didn't know anyone else

here, except Zack. No doubt that was what he meant!

She smiled up at him, aware that people were eyeing them curiously. 'I intend getting out of here the first opportunity I get—'

'Merry? Merry Baker? It is you, isn't it?'

Merry froze once more. Not only did someone else at this party know her, and her name, but she knew them too, recognised that voice! It had been about nineteen years since she had last heard it, but it was a voice she would never forget.

'I thought so,' Karen Jacobs drawled derisively as Merry turned slowly to face her. 'You haven't changed a bit.' Her gaze swept over Merry's appearance. 'Same hairstyle. Same dress,' she added pointedly.

Karen obviously hadn't changed, either, she had always been a first-class bitch. Albeit a beautiful one, with an eye for style—which was probably why she'd recognised the dress! It was a talent that had made her editor of one of the top fashion magazines. A tall, willowy blonde, the other woman was as slender as she had always been. Although years ago her hair had been long, now it was cut short, framing the perfect beauty of her face, her eyes deeply blue, and fringed by long, dark lashes.

Merry's eyes turned to the man standing awkwardly at Karen's side; he was tall and dark, almost too good-looking, and there was a weakness about his mouth and in his deep brown eyes that couldn't quite meet Merry's. Here was one person, at least, who would rather not have renewed the acquaintance!

Zack merely looked puzzled by the couple, frowning as he stood slightly on the outside of the group, watching them with narrowed eyes. Like a spectator at a play. Except Merry didn't intend letting him remain that way; he was the one who had brought her here in the first place!

'Darling.' She curved her arm intimately through the crook of his, pulling him gently, but firmly, to her side. 'I would like to introduce you to Karen and Roger Jacobs.'

'Zack and I already know each other,' Karen told her coolly.

Merry nodded. 'But I doubt he realises that you are the younger sister of my sister-in-law,' she said lightly, shooting Zack a warning look as he looked stunned by this information.

As well he might. Karen and Roger Jacobs were as different in lifestyle to Merry as chalk was to cheese; the other couple, with their fine clothes and rich jewellery, were obviously far wealthier than schoolmistress Merry. It hadn't had to be that way, of course, but the price for remaining a part of her family had been far too high for her to pay.

'How *are* Glenda and Stephen?' she prompted Roger, trying to draw him into the conversation; he and Karen hadn't been married when she'd known them all those years ago, but Merry hadn't missed the diamond-studded wedding ring on Karen's left hand. 'And my mother and father, of course,' she added tonelessly.

She couldn't mention Glenda and Stephen without bringing her parents into the picture too. A dutiful son, Stephen, her older brother, had married the woman of their mother's choice. Merry had no reason to doubt that Stephen had since continued to do exactly as he was told. The two of them had been close when they were children, but their differences had become glaring when they were older. 'Dutiful' was not a word that could ever be applied to Merry—or to anything that she did!

Roger didn't look at all happy with this situation. 'They are well,' he answered abruptly, obviously uncomfortable with the whole conversation.

Merry couldn't claim to be exactly thrilled about it herself. As for Zack, he wasn't saying anything, but stood taking in everything that was being discussed. And formulating some questions of his own, no doubt!

'How is your—what did you have, by the way?' Karen raised supercilious brows as she looked at Merry. 'You'll have to excuse us, Zack,' she told him throatily, resting her hand briefly on his arm in a gesture of intimacy. 'As a family, we're always shamelessly lax about keeping in touch with one another.' She gave a tinkling laugh.

Merry returned the other woman's gaze coldly. She hadn't considered this woman part of her family nineteen years ago, and she certainly didn't do so now. Dani was her family now, her only family...

'I have a daughter,' she told the other couple flatly. 'How about you? Do you have children?'

'Certainly not,' Karen dismissed disgustedly. 'I can't imagine anything worse than a screaming little brat hanging onto my ankles. And pregnancy seems to play havoc with a woman's figure,' she concluded bitchily, the fitted red dress she wore showing not an ounce of superfluous flesh on her body.

Zack moved at last, putting his arm possessively about Merry's waist as he drew her closer to his side. 'Let me be the first to assure you that pregnancy did absolutely nothing negative to Merry's body,' he stated, his own eyes challenging now as he looked at Karen. 'She's perfect exactly as she is.'

While she was grateful for his support, at the same time Merry really didn't need the bitchy Karen to get any bitchier—and Zack's remark was sure to make her so!

'Do Glenda and Stephen have children now?' Merry put in quickly.

'No,' the other woman rejoined abruptly. 'Glenda is as averse to pregnancy as I am.'

Merry somehow doubted that; an heir for the Baker family had been paramount in her mother's plans. But it seemed there wasn't one...

'What did happen to that ghastly man you were involved with?' Karen was being deliberately provocative. 'And his equally ghastly wife?' she went on, before Merry could make any reply.

Merry felt herself pale. She hadn't known Jeff was married when she'd fallen so recklessly in love with him. Not that the fact changed anything; he *had* been married, and it had been a marriage he'd had no intention of leaving. Certainly not for a pregnant eighteen-year-old!

She opened her mouth to reply to the insult—only to find Zack had got there first.

'Family reminiscences can be so amusing, can't they?' he put in lightly, the strength of his arm about

Merry not light at all! 'We must remember to invite you all to the wedding.'

'Wedding?' Karen echoed sharply, eyes narrowed maliciously as she looked at the two of them suspiciously.

'Yes—our wedding,' Merry heard herself confirm—and then almost gasped out loud as she realised what she had said.

'Well, well, well,' Karen drawled speculatively. 'Could it be that we hear the patter of tiny feet once again?' she asked, looking Merry up and down.

Merry had moved instinctively to slap the other woman for the deliberate jibe; Karen's implication was unmistakable: Merry would only be able to catch a husband like Zack by becoming pregnant! But again Zack was quicker than her, his hand tightly grasping her arm before it could swing upwards and her hand could make contact with the other woman's mocking, smiling face.

The pleasant expression on Zack's face didn't so much as waver, although only a fool could have missed the steely glint in his eyes. 'Funny you should mention that—' his voice was silkily soft—though that silk barely covered the steel beneath, '—we were talking only yesterday about the possibility of getting ourselves a dog once we're married!'

Karen looked startled, momentarily disconcerted. 'A dog?'

'A dog,' Merry concurred, recovering quickly from the other woman's insults; she was no longer an immature teenager, she was a mother, with a responsible job. She had made a success of her life, she realised, despite her family. 'Cats make Zack sneeze,' she continued conversationally, shooting him a grateful look from beneath lowered lashes; the worst thing she could do would be to reduce herself to Karen's level.

'They most certainly—*atishoo!*' Right on cue, Zack sneezed. 'Please excuse me,' he apologised blandly. 'I—*atishoo!*' He sneezed again. 'It seems it's not only the furry kind that have that effect on me,' he added, his expression one of complete innocence.

Roger shot Karen an apprehensive glance as her face tightened furiously. 'I think we should go and circulate, darling.' He took a firm hold of his wife's arm. 'I'm sure we've monopolised enough of Zack's attention for one evening.'

Karen visibly forced herself to relax, her mouth curving into a fixed smile, although her eyes remained glacially hard. 'It was wonderful to see you again,' she said insincerely. 'Your parents will be pleased to know you've done so well for yourself,' she told Merry haughtily.

Merry replied with stony silence. Her parents, her mother, at least, had shown no interest in her over the last nineteen years, and she had no reason to suppose this chance meeting tonight would change any of that. In fact, she didn't want it to—could imagine nothing worse than having to deal with her mother once again!

'Nice to see you again, Roger.' She moved to kiss him lightly on the cheek, smiling at him reassuringly as he gave her an appeasing look. Roger always had been the nicer of this couple! Although weak, very weak...

'You really are looking wonderful, Merry,' he braved his wife's wrath to tell her warmly.

Not so weak after all, Merry acknowledged lightly, returning his smile.

'I always did like you in that dress,' Karen added as her own parting comment.

Merry gave a rueful shake of her head as she watched the other couple walk away. The rich and the beautiful. How sad they really were.

'Meow,' Zack murmured laughingly in her ear.

Zack!

What on earth must he be thinking of her now? Not only were her family awful, but she was a single mother whose lover had been a married man!

Merry had been so young, not much older than Dani was now. Although she had always loved her father, it had been her mother who'd made the decisions, her mother who had decided on the schools her two children would attend, on the universities they eventually went to. She had even chosen Stephen's wife for him. While Merry's father had been a good man, a kind, loving man, he had always meekly acquiesced to his wife's decisions, aware that she was the one who held the pursestrings.

Merry hadn't realised it at the time—although she had had plenty of time in the years that followed!—but at eighteen she had been looking for a man who was strong and dependable, a man who knew who he was, and where he was going. Jeff had seemed all of those things to Merry's inexperienced eye—but ultimately he had proved he was weaker than her father and brother, a man who used his marriage like a shield while he indulged in numerous affairs that could never go anywhere because he already had a wife! Merry had only learnt the full truth of that when she'd found herself pregnant with his child...

But Zack didn't know any of that, had merely been told by the bitchy Karen that the father of her baby had been a married man. A man who obviously hadn't stood by her when she needed him.

What must Zack be thinking?

He moved to stand in front of her, his hands moving to tenderly cup either side of her face as he tilted it up to his. 'You do realise,' he told her huskily, 'that I intend keeping you to the statement?'

Which statement? There had been so many in the last ten minutes—and none of them complimentary to her!

'The wedding,' Zack explained teasingly as she looked blank. 'I could sue you for breach of contract if you try to back out of marrying me now!'

He could sue her? What did *she* possibly possess that he could sue her for?

Nothing, came the immediate answer. But Zack was telling her, more succinctly than ever, that what he had heard in the last ten minutes hadn't changed how he felt about her at all...!

Merry laughed, a light, relieved laugh. Of course she had no intention of marrying him, but at the same time she didn't want him to think badly of her either. And he didn't...

'That's better.' He spoke his satisfaction at her

laugh, his hands leaving her cheeks as he reached down and placed one of her own hands firmly in his. 'And now I believe it's time to get ourselves a drink and circulate.'

'Circulate' meant accompanying Zack as he spoke briefly with every person in the room, Zack charming and assured as he did so. It quickly became obvious that not only did his guests like him, they trusted and respected him too.

Zack Kingston, Merry realised dazedly, *was* a strong, dependable man, a man who knew who he was and where he was going...

Oh, help!

CHAPTER EIGHT

'I WAS eighteen when I met Jeff,' Merry told Zack a couple of hours later, when the two of them were sitting in a quiet restaurant together enjoying a late supper. Although Merry's appetite deserted her the moment she began to talk about that disastrous relationship nineteen years ago. A relationship that had ultimately changed the whole of her life...

She had been eighteen, the daughter of a wealthy family, beginning her art degree. The whole world had been at her feet, her future choices unlimited. Then she'd met Jeff.

'You really don't have to tell me any of this, you know,' Zack assured her. 'I think I know enough about human nature by now to realise that Karen Jacobs is not a nice woman.' He paused. 'That her version of events is coloured by her own unhappiness.'

Merry's eyes widened. 'What makes you say that?' Karen had struck her as a woman comfortable with her own success.

Zack sipped at his wine, his first alcoholic drink of the evening. He had stuck to drinking orange juice throughout the cocktail party, explaining quietly to Merry that it was work and not pleasure. Most of the guest list had been made up of

Thorndyke authors, the rest of them television, newspaper, and magazine personalities—hence Karen's invitation at all. Despite the impression Karen had tried to give of a greater intimacy between herself and Zack, Merry knew which version she believed!

'Merry, you have so much more than Karen does. Oh, yes, you do,' he confirmed as she tried to protest. 'Bullies rarely pick on people they actually consider inferior to them, even though it might seem that they do. It's invariably someone who really possesses something they wish they had.'

'I can assure you,' Merry snorted, 'I have nothing Karen could possibly want!'

'How about independence? You obviously broke away from family ties. And personal success—you couldn't look and behave the way you do if you weren't perfectly satisfied with your life exactly as it is— What is it?' he pounced sharply as she pondered this last comment.

'Nothing.' She forced a brightness into her smile. 'None of us can claim to have everything we want.' She excused her brief moment of regret. She had everything she *needed*...

'That's true,' Zack acknowledged slowly. 'I thought my life was running along quite nicely—until I met you and realised it had a damned great hole in it!'

'Zack,' she warned reprovingly.

'Okay, don't believe me,' he said. 'But David is about as close as I've ever had to someone I could sit down and talk to the way I do with you. And as we both know, that isn't the same thing at all!'

She did know. Close as she and Dani were, friends as well as mother and daughter, that latter relationship precluded her from talking to Dani about some things. Besides, there was a generation gap that wasn't there between Zack and herself.

Help again!

'You're a successful woman in your own right, Merry, through your own endeavours and not through a family connection,' Zack continued determinedly. 'You also have something else that Karen and her sister, your sister-in-law do not have.'

Now Merry was very puzzled. What could she possibly have—Zack? He surely didn't mean himself?

Had that intimate hand on his arm meant something, after all? There was no doubting that Karen was a beautiful woman, and—

'I have no idea what you're thinking now.' Zack cut in on her racing thoughts. 'From the expression on your face, I don't think I want to know, either! I was talking about Dani, Merry,' he explained as she looked at him uncomprehendingly once again. 'You have a child.'

'But—'

'I was watching Roger's face during that part of the conversation.' Zack shook his head. 'Karen may have chosen not to have children; I accept that part of it. But I have a feeling it's something else completely with your sister-in-law. Roger looked taken aback when Karen claimed her sister didn't want children either, which leads me to believe that she probably can't have any... Does that sound feasible to you?' he asked thoughtfully.

Merry remembered her mother's glee when Stephen had married Glenda; her wish had been that the young couple provided her with grandchildren as quickly as possible. And Merry's brother had always been so dutiful...

'How sad,' Merry sighed—and sincerely meant it. Glenda was too much like Karen for her and Merry ever to have been friends, but even so she couldn't help feeling for the other woman, if what Zack suggested was true. It *did* sound feasible.

Her own life would have been so much bleaker without Dani in it. Less complicated too, she accepted that, but she wouldn't change her life for Karen's or Glenda's. Which was exactly what Zack had been talking about all the time...

'Will you see any of your family again?' Zack prompted gently as he watched the emotions flickering across her face.

Merry gave him a startled look. 'Why on earth should I? One chance meeting with the sister of my sister-in-law—the first in nineteen years, I might add—' she told him hurriedly—one step into *his* life and she had been thrown into the company of people she hadn't seen since she was a teenager, whom she'd had no wish to see during that time, either! '—gives me no interest in seeing again the family who totally rejected me and my unborn child!' The last came out slightly bitterly, although it came as a surprise to Merry that she should still feel that way.

She didn't know what reaction she had expected from her parents on learning of her pregnancy, but it certainly hadn't been the one she had got. Of course, her brother, Stephen, weak as usual, hadn't questioned their decision.

'That's what happened, isn't it?' Zack said understandingly. 'You broke the acceptable code, and so they threw you out.' His mouth tightened grimly at the thought.

'Oh, I could have stayed,' Merry informed him with barely concealed distaste. 'All I had to do to remain part of the Baker family was destroy my own child before it was born! It's ironic, really,' she went on. 'That unwanted grandchild is now the only one they have.'

'Their only heir,' he confirmed. 'You didn't tell me you were *that* Baker,' he tacked on playfully, reminding her of her comment when she'd realised he was the Kingston who owned Thorndyke Books.

But she knew exactly what he meant by his remark; the Baker family were old money—owned property all over the world, had shares in numerous companies. Her father had even been the one to change *his* surname when he'd married her mother; as the only Baker heir of her generation, her mother had had no intention of relinquishing hers.

But the name, and all that went with it, had meant nothing to Merry, and she didn't want the family inheritance for Dani either...

'You didn't ask,' she replied. 'And Dani may be the only heir,' she added tightly, 'but she has nothing to do with the family!'

Zack persisted. 'She may not feel that way. And Karen strikes me as a troublemaker...'

He was right, of course; Karen had always liked to stir things up and then sit back and watch the situation develop! To mention this evening's accidental meeting with Merry to her family would benefit no one. Which was exactly why Karen *would* do such a thing, of course!

'What a mess,' Merry muttered irritably.

'And all my fault,' Zack put in ruefully.

She looked at him sharply, feeling the colour in her cheeks. 'I didn't say that.'

'You didn't have to,' he responded, reaching across the table to take one of her hands in his. 'I can tell exactly what you're thinking. Merry, I'm really sorry this has happened, but at the same time I suggest you let Dani make her own mind up about this if—or when—the time comes. She's your daughter; she'll know the right thing to do.'

Dani *was* her daughter, and she hoped that she had been a good mother to her, that she had instilled all the right values in her. It was just that the Baker family could be so powerful if they chose to be.

Not with her daughter, they couldn't! Dani might only be eighteen, but she had her own code of moral values, a sense of what was right and what was wrong—though a few days ago Merry *had* made the erroneous assumption that Dani was pregnant with David Kingston's child...!

No! Dani was a sensible young lady, would never do anything to hurt someone else, would never be taken in by the lavish lifestyle the Baker family had to offer. Dani simply wasn't impetuous.

Merry wasn't quite so sure about that when they arrived back at the house a short time later and Dani dreamily greeted her at the front door with the words, 'Mum, I've met the man I'm going to marry!'

Not another one! What was *wrong* with everyone all of a sudden?

This was just too much!

CHAPTER NINE

'I *WAS* mistaken.' Zack's voice came from behind Merry. 'David *is* as impatient as I am!'

Merry wasn't in the mood for levity. This whole situation was becoming ridiculous. 'Dani.' She spoke firmly to her daughter. 'I suggest we talk about this once Zack has left.'

'Oh, hi, Zack.' Dani looked at him as he stood in the shadows behind her mother. 'I didn't see you there.' She looked a little embarrassed at having been quite so open in his presence. 'I'll leave the two of you to finish your evening,' she apologised. 'I just wanted to... Night, Mum.' She bent to kiss Merry on the cheek. 'Zack.' She ran up the stairs, not dwelling on her outspokenness.

Merry didn't move. What was wrong with everybody. Had they put something in the water? What, for goodness' sake? Because suddenly everyone around her wanted to get married!

Zack strolled past her into the house, turning back when Merry still didn't move. 'It *was* David she was talking about, wasn't it?' he queried.

Merry shot him an impatient glance. 'Unless she met someone else before or after the film—of course it was David!' She marched determinedly into the house after slamming the door behind her. 'What is it with your family?' she demanded accusingly. 'You have to leave, Zack. You and your nephew. You're turning our lives upside down. We were fine as we were. We don't need—*I* don't need—' Where had these tears come from, cascading hotly down her cheeks, making speech impossible, and her whole body tremble with reaction?

'Merry!' Zack enveloped her in warm, comforting arms, holding her against his chest.

This was exactly what she didn't want! But she was too upset, too tired, too emotionally fraught to fight against it at this moment. She had been fighting too long, alone against so many obstacles. Right now she simply didn't have the strength to fight against the protection Zack's arms gave her against those obstacles. It was all too easy just to give herself up to being the one who was looked after for a change, rather than the one who did the looking after.

She could barely see Zack as she looked up at him through her tears, had no idea how vulnerable she looked. But she did feel the gentle pressure of Zack's lips against hers, the way her body melted into his as she returned his kiss, and not gently at all.

She needed—oh, God, at this moment she needed Zack! To be kissed by him. Not to have to think, if only for a brief time. Bliss!

She had never been kissed like this in her life before!

Zack's lips wreaked havoc on the softness of hers, his arms like steel bands as he moulded her body to the hard contours of his. Once again Merry was amazed at how well their bodies fitted together, even if he was too tall…

She was babbling again—but in her head this time!

Her neck arched as Zack's lips trailed a fiery path to the creamy hollows the black dress left bare, one of his hands lightly caressing the full upthrust of her breast, her nipple pulsating with pleasure beneath the silky material.

'Oh, Zack…!' she groaned weakly, knowing that if this continued much longer she was going to be completely lost. Dani was upstairs—

Dear Lord, Dani! She couldn't behave in this wanton fashion with her daughter only feet away, albeit up the stairs and in her own bedroom with the door firmly closed. Dreaming about David, no doubt!

Zack released Merry reluctantly as she pulled away. 'Don't look so upset, Merry,' he chided. 'It was only a kiss.'

Only a kiss? She didn't think so! The truth of the matter was, she was falling in love with this man. If she wasn't already in love with him! And *that* terrified the life out of her…!

'That isn't what I'm upset about.' She retreated into anger. 'You came here the other day, insisting that my daughter couldn't marry your nephew; now I suggest you go home and tell him the same thing.'

As she warmed to the subject, she really did feel angry. Zack had made things worse by coming here two days ago; until that time Dani hadn't so much as given David a second glance—now it appeared she was in love with him!

'They are both far too young to think about getting married,' she snapped. 'And Dani wouldn't even have thought about taking David seriously if you hadn't piqued her interest,' she accused, eyes brightly green.

'Merry—'

'Don't you "Merry" me in that patronising tone!'

'Another fault to add to the long list?' Zack arched blond brows, his hair falling endearingly onto his forehead.

But Merry only felt more irritated as she noticed his tousled hair—it had been her fingers running through it that had caused the disarray! 'Just the truth,' she bit out coldly. 'You have only complicated my life—'

'Isn't that better than just emotionally skimming along the surface?' he suggested softly.

She became very still. 'Exactly what do you mean by that remark?' But she knew; she *knew*!

Zack drew in a deep breath, slowly releasing it again. 'Merry, I know what you're trying to do—and I'm not going to fight you,' he added quickly as she went to speak. 'I care about you very much, Merry, and I know I've been bulldozing you the last few days. I also accept that it isn't working, that I'm only succeeding in upsetting you. It's my way. See what I want—and go for it. It probably has something to do with that arrogance you once accused me of,' he admitted.

He was trying to lighten up now, and in a way he was succeeding. Because it was his previous remark that had hit her with the force of a sledgehammer. Emotionally skimming on the surface of life...

Was that what she had been doing the last nineteen years…?

The first few years after Dani's birth had been hard, looking after a small child, working hard on her degree course, living on a small allowance. By the time Dani began school herself, Merry had been ready to begin her teaching career. Since then, the years had simply flown by, filled with Dani and her job, and her personal life put almost on permanent hold; even the few dates she had accepted had always been with men with whom she had a mutual interest, but whom she hadn't found particular attractive. Emotionally skimming, Zack had called it…

''Merry, you know that I want you in my life.' Zack lightly gripped the tops of her arms. 'But I want you there permanently, as my wife, and I won't accept anything less.'

He was so different from Jeff it was difficult to take in. The last thing Jeff had wanted was to marry her; Zack wouldn't accept anything less…

'I want a white wedding,' he continued with assurance. 'The walking down the aisle and the ''till death us do part'' bits. I would like us to have a child together. But you have to want all those things too. And until you do, perhaps it's better if I stay out of your way,' he concluded heavily. 'I can love and cherish you, but until you love me in return you're only going to view my actions with suspicion—and great caution. I don't want that. I don't want to go on causing you distress, either.'

He was leaving her life! As quickly as he had come into it, he was leaving!

'I'll have a chat with David,' he promised, releasing her, stepping back, the happiness gone from his face now, his expression as grim as the first day he had knocked on her door. 'See what plans he and Dani have. If any,' he added self-disgustedly. 'I won't jump to any conclusions this time!'

And neither would Merry! She had totally misjudged the whole situation last time, although common sense—and her knowledge of Dani—had thankfully kicked into action.

But that was for later, once Zack had gone. Because he *was* leaving. And he wasn't coming back. There was nothing she could do or say that would stop him—because she couldn't say the words he wanted to hear! Maybe it was emotionally skimming, but at least this way no one had been able to hurt her in all these years...

Once Zack was out of her life again, she would be able to return to that.

Wouldn't she...?

CHAPTER TEN

'I KNOW I shouldn't, Mum, but I feel really nervous,' Dani told Merry as they stood outside the huge oak door that fronted the imposing house.

Merry shot her daughter a sympathetic glance. She couldn't claim to be feeling exactly relaxed about this herself. But it wouldn't do for *both* of them to admit to feeling nervous!

Zack had been proved correct in his observation that Karen appeared to him to be a woman who liked to create trouble! He had been right about several other things too, Merry had realised in the week since he'd left her, but those other things she had pushed to the back of her mind, deciding that what they were dealing with now was more important for the moment. After all, tomorrow *was* another day...

Not even a day had passed from the time she had met Karen again to when she'd received a telephone call from her father—she had vowed at that moment to become ex-directory! But the call had to come from her father, of course, because, as they all knew, Merry would have simply replaced the receiver on hearing the sound of her mother's voice. And would have still gone ex-directory!

Her father was another matter completely; Merry had always been close to him during her childhood, and had received no ultimatums from *him* when she'd told her parents of her pregnancy. What her mother hadn't known then, and probably still didn't know, was that her father had visited Merry shortly after she'd given birth to Dani, that he had helped her financially too, during those first few difficult years of studying and being a single mother. It was as much as he'd been able to do when her mother had refused to even have Merry's name mentioned in the house.

She knew her mother had put her father up to the telephone call inviting herself and Dani to dinner; he wouldn't have dared to do it without her mother's consent.

Dinner. Just the four of them, her father had assured her. With no hidden agenda. She had never known her mother *not* to have one, but this time it wasn't so hidden; Dani was the only Baker grandchild, and her grandmother wanted to meet her.

In which case, in total agreement with Zack over this, Merry had felt it was Dani's choice...

Which was the reason they were now standing outside the front door of the Baker residence. Merry hadn't made the same mistake this evening of wearing the classic black dress that had earned her such ridicule from Karen last week! Her dress tonight, newly bought, was the same deep emerald colour of her eyes, and it fitted the tininess of her slender figure perfectly. It might be so in real life, but Merry wouldn't look like the poor relation this evening!

'Your grandfather is wonderful, Dani,' she told her daughter softly. 'My mother—' She stopped, at a loss for words where her mother was concerned—

where *any* mother who could reject her own daughter under such circumstances was concerned. She had tried several times during the last week to describe Mrs Baker to Dani, but the truth simply wouldn't do; she owed her mother nothing, but Dani's relationship with her was a completely different matter.

'Don't keep worrying about it, Mum.' Dani squeezed her hand reassuringly. 'I simply want to meet them both. I'm curious, that's all. I don't expect to feel much else,' she added.

Merry's first thought, on seeing her mother again for the first time in nineteen years, was that time hadn't been kind to her. The face that had once been regally beautiful had become pinched and bitter; Eleanor Baker looked all of her sixty-three years!

Merry's father had fared slightly better, tall, and still strikingly handsome in his black dinner suit, wings of grey at his temples in hair otherwise as dark as Merry's own. It was so good to see him again!

'Merry, darling.' He moved forward to hug her. 'You look wonderful,' he told her warmly.

She blinked back the tears, proudly pulling Dani to her side. She *was* so proud of Dani, felt she was the single most perfect thing she had ever done in her life. 'This is my daughter, Dani—short for Daniella.' The last was added slightly defensively as she looked across the room to where her mother stood, looking at them all so aloofly.

The house itself hadn't changed at all since Merry's childhood, still the show-piece of the woman who owned it, the deep red and gold decor

somehow seeming to reflect Eleanor Baker's cold-
ness rather than casting the warm effect that it
should have.

'Named for your father, of course.' Her mother
spoke for the first time since their arrival, a voice
well-remembered from the last time Merry and her
mother had spoken: cold and slightly condescend-
ing.

How her mother must hate having to do this,
Merry realised sadly, almost feeling sorry for that.
Almost... Too much had been said and done in the
past for her ever to completely forgive Eleanor.

Merry's head went back. 'Of course,' she confirmed in a clipped voice, remembering the proud
look on her father's face the day he'd realised she
had named her daughter after him.

'In that case, my dear,' Eleanor spoke directly to
her granddaughter, 'I shall call you Daniella.'

Dani returned her look with unblinking eyes. 'I
would rather you didn't. My name is Dani,' she replied clearly.

Merry looked at the two women, the one so much
older now, but having lost none of her imperious-
ness, the other poised on the brink of womanhood—
and her expression turned to one of amazement as
she saw for the first time that Dani had her grandmother's regal bearing, if none of her snobbery, and
a definite will of her own! Her mother, Merry realised with some amusement as she began to relax for
the first time in days, had met her match in her
granddaughter!

'Very well,' Eleanor accepted after several stunned
seconds. 'I'm sure it's a very pretty name.'

'I've always thought so,' Dani agreed.

The initial clash between grandmother and grand-daughter, in which Dani had undoubtedly been the winner, set the tone for the rest of the evening, with Merry's mother avoiding any subjects that might be cause for controversy. Including that of Merry's supposed engagement to Zack Kingston... Karen was sure to have mentioned that little fact to the family as well, Merry was sure. But it was never mentioned.

In fact, the whole evening was more pleasant than Merry could possibly have hoped for. What had seemed to her like a huge mountain to climb had turned out to be nothing more than a small molehill. She would never forgive or forget the way her mother had let her down all those years ago, in fact she might never see her mother again after this evening, but it really didn't matter to her any more. She had faced her mother and felt nothing but a slight sense of pity—for all that her mother could have had, which instead she had so wantonly given up.

'Whew, what a dragon.' Dani's chuckled remark, on their way home shortly after ten o'clock, seemed to echo Merry's thoughts. 'Grandpa is a poppet, though,' she added with real affection, having fallen quite easily into calling him such, while Eleanor had very firmly remained Eleanor!

Merry eyed her daughter ruefully. She needn't have worried on that score either; Dani knew exactly who she was—and wasn't! 'You do realise what tonight was all about, don't you?'

'Of course.' Dani wrinkled her nose inelegantly.

'They wanted to look me over, see if I'm good enough to be a Baker.'

Merry laughed at her daughter's forthright summing up of the evening. Dani was right, of course; Merry probably just wouldn't have put it quite that bluntly. 'Do you think you passed?' she teased.

'Who cares?' Dani dismissed.

Exactly—who cared any more? That particular nemesis was well and truly faced as far as Merry was concerned, and Dani wasn't about to let it become one for her.

Dani reached out and squeezed her arm briefly. 'You've been a wonderful mother to me,' she told her huskily. 'The best family anyone could ever wish for.'

Merry swallowed hard. 'Thank you.'

'I'm glad you decided to name me after Grandpa, though. He loves you, and you obviously love him very much.'

'Not as much as I love you,' Merry told her softly.

'What a lucky pair we are,' Dani pronounced with satisfaction. 'And as for my surname; that's going to be totally irrelevant once I'm married to David,' she said happily.

Dani had remained firm in the announcement she had made almost a week ago. Having now met David several times, Merry agreed with Zack that his nephew looked nothing like him, but in other ways he was so like his uncle it brought a lump into her throat just to be in the same room with him.

'Have the two of you decided on a date for the wedding yet?' she probed gently.

Dani shrugged. 'Some time after we've both got our degrees, and before we start medical school.'

Merry had been included in several conversations with the young couple, and she knew that their ultimate aim was to open up a medical practice together—Kingston and Kingston. They seemed to have progressed a long way in a week, but, as Merry knew only too well herself, it *was* possible to fall in love in the space of a second, not to mention in three days...!

'Isn't he sweet,' Dani murmured dreamily at her side. 'I told David how nervous I felt about this evening,' she explained at Merry's questioning look, 'and he's sat here and waited for me to come home.' She pointed to the colourful Mini parked in front of their home.

Merry's own gaze went past the Mini to the Jaguar stationed in front of it. *She* hadn't told Zack she was nervous about seeing her parents again—in fact she hadn't spoken to him for six days—but it looked as if he had guessed her feelings for himself, and decided to follow his nephew's example. He had waited for her to come home, too!

CHAPTER ELEVEN

How Merry's heart ached just at the sight of him!

She had inwardly acknowledged to herself this week how much she was missing him, but face to face with him like this——! She ached, too, to know the warmth of his smile, the deep huskiness of his laugh, the warm strength of his arms, to hear him tell her again that he loved her...

'Zack,' she greeted him tensely, having locked her car door and turned to find him standing on the pavement beside her.

But she had known he was there, had felt him there.

'Mum, David and I are just going for a drive,' Dani called out to her as she got into the car beside David.

Zack looked at Merry closely, searchingly. 'Is everything okay?' he prompted softly as his nephew and Dani drove away.

'Why shouldn't it be?' Merry dismissed flippantly. 'Dani and I have just come back from dinner, that's all.'

His deep blue gaze remained fixed on her face. 'I know where you've been, Merry,' he confirmed gently. 'David told me. I had to come; I feel responsible.'

Responsible? She didn't want him to feel that—it was the last emotion she wanted from him!

She had thought so much about him this last week—had hardly been able to think about anything else. Thoughts of Zack, and how she felt about him, had even lessened the importance of dinner with her parents this evening. But she had known she had to get that out of the way, for Dani's sake, before she made any move to see Zack.

And now he had come to see her...

What did they do now? If Dani and David had stayed then they could all have gone into the house for coffee, but—

'Invite me in, Merry,' Zack demanded gruffly.

Now that he was here this was all going too fast for her. What if—?

Zack barely waited for the door to close behind them before gathering her up into his arms. 'I've missed you!' he groaned, his face buried in the scented softness of her hair.

She had missed him too. God, how she had missed him. He was deep inside her heart now, and she couldn't seem to get him out. In fact, she had decided in these last days without him that she didn't want to!

'What did you say?' Zack had become very still, raising his head to look down at her with eyes that had gone cobalt blue.

What had she said? She hadn't— She couldn't have—

'I love you, Zack.' The words came out clear and firm this time.

And she was the one who had said them. Not once, but twice!

'You love me...?' He seemed totally astounded by her admission. *He* was astounded; she didn't even seem to have control over what she said any more!

'Yes,' she confirmed with certainty. 'And there is no responsibility to be felt about this evening by anyone. I realise now that I should have done it years ago.' She shook her head. 'All I can see them as now is two elderly people who have lived their lives by a code, imposed by other people as well as themselves. And because of that they missed out on their granddaughter growing up. I...' She hesitated momentarily. 'I've lived my own life by a certain code these last nineteen years too. It's a code that hasn't allowed people close enough to be able to hurt me. "Emotionally skimming", I think you called it,' she remembered ruefully.'

'Merry—'

'No, let me finish, Zack?' she asked softly. 'Because I've stopped skimming. What's left is a very emotional woman, a woman who wants that white wedding, the walking down the aisle *and* the "till death us do part" bits.' The tears in her eyes blurred her vision, but she knew Zack was still there, could feel him there. 'But only if *you're* the man waiting at the end of that aisle for me. Zack, will you marry me?' Oh, *help*. She quaked inwardly as she heard herself say those last four words.

His arms tightened about her. 'I'll even let you plan the wedding—as long as you make it soon!' he grated.

She didn't care how soon it was. She had been without him this last week—and she had absolutely hated it. She loved this man, every caring inch of him!

'Do you mind if we convert the top of my house into a studio for you *after* we're married? I really don't want to wait until the work is completed—' Zack looked down at her as she gasped. 'I remember you once told me that no one has everything they want, so I asked Dani what it was *you* wanted—and she told me you had always wanted a place of your own where you can paint full time.' He paused and smiled. 'Your wish will be granted, my love.'

Candid, *wonderful* Dani!

'I would like us to have a child of our own, too,' she told him almost shyly. To finally be given the studio she had always wanted would be wonderful, but at the moment she could imagine nothing more exciting than the two of them having a baby of their own to love and care for.

'Remembering your inability to take the pill—I told you I would store that away for future reference!' he joked '—and the way I find it difficult to keep my hands of you, I think that it's highly likely!' he said. 'There's absolutely no reason why you can't paint *and* have our baby, my darling,' he assured her lovingly. 'Together we can do anything!'

Together... It wasn't something she had ever known before. But it sounded and felt wonderful!

And she knew, with Zack, it always would be...

HARLEQUIN  PRESENTS®

THE BARONS

One sister, three brothers— who will inherit, and will they all find lovers?

Jonas is approaching his eighty-fifth birthday, and he's decided it's time to choose the heir of his sprawling ranch, Espada. He has three ruggedly good-looking sons, Gage, Travis and Slade, and a beautiful stepdaughter, Caitlin.

Who will receive Baron's bequest? As the Baron brothers and their sister discover, there's more at stake than Espada. For love also has its part to play in deciding their futures....

Enjoy Gage's story:
Marriage on the Edge
Harlequin Presents #2027, May 1999

And in August, get to know Travis a whole lot better in
More than a Mistress
Harlequin Presents #2045

Available wherever Harlequin books are sold.

HARLEQUIN®
Makes any time special ™

Look us up on-line at: http://www.romance.net   HPBARON

If you enjoyed what you just read,
then we've got an offer you can't resist!

Take 2 bestselling love stories FREE!

Plus get a FREE surprise gift!

Clip this page and mail it to Harlequin Reader Service®

IN U.S.A.
3010 Walden Ave.
P.O. Box 1867
Buffalo, N.Y. 14240-1867

IN CANADA
P.O. Box 609
Fort Erie, Ontario
L2A 5X3

YES! Please send me 2 free Harlequin Presents® novels and my free surprise gift. Then send me 6 brand-new novels every month, which I will receive months before they're available in stores. In the U.S.A., bill me at the bargain price of $3.12 plus 25¢ delivery per book and applicable sales tax, if any*. In Canada, bill me at the bargain price of $3.49 plus 25¢ delivery per book and applicable taxes**. That's the complete price and a savings of over 10% off the cover prices—what a great deal! I understand that accepting the 2 free books and gift places me under no obligation ever to buy any books. I can always return a shipment and cancel at any time. Even if I never buy another book from Harlequin, the 2 free books and gift are mine to keep forever. So why not take us up on our invitation. You'll be glad you did!

106 HEN CNER
306 HEN CNES

Name _____ (PLEASE PRINT)

Address _____ Apt.#

City _____ State/Prov. _____ Zip/Postal Code

* Terms and prices subject to change without notice. Sales tax applicable in N.Y.
** Canadian residents will be charged applicable provincial taxes and GST.
   All orders subject to approval. Offer limited to one per household.
   ® are registered trademarks of Harlequin Enterprises Limited.

PRES99   ©1998 Harlequin Enterprises Limited

HARLEQUIN PRESENTS®

Passion™

Looking for stories that **sizzle?**
Wanting a read that has a little
extra **spice?**

Harlequin Presents® is thrilled to
bring you romances that turn up
the **heat!**

Every other month throughout
1999 there'll be a **PRESENTS
PASSION** book by one of your
favorite authors.

In May 1999 don't miss
***The Millionaire's Mistress* by Miranda Lee**
Harlequin Presents® #2026

*Pick up a **PRESENTS PASSION**—
where **seduction** is guaranteed!*

Available wherever Harlequin books are sold.

HARLEQUIN®

Makes any time special™

Look us up on-line at: http://www.romance.net   HPPAS2

THE PERFECT SINNER

The Crighton family saga continues in this riveting
novel from *New York Times* bestselling author

Prominent lawyer Max Crighton has it all—money, power, the perfect
home life. But he's putting it all at risk by his reckless and
dangerous behavior.

Then Max is brutally attacked. And the man who comes home from
the hospital is a stranger to his wife, Maddy, to his children and to
himself. Has the perfect sinner truly repented?

"Women everywhere will find pieces of themselves
in Jordan's characters."
—*Publishers Weekly*

MIRA

On sale mid-June 1999 wherever paperbacks are sold!

Look us up on-line at: http://www.mirabooks.com   MPJS15

HARLEQUIN  PRESENTS®

Jarrett, Jonathan and Jordan are

An exhilarating new miniseries by favorite author

CAROLE MORTIMER

The Hunter brothers are handsome, wealthy and
determinedly single—until each meets the woman
of his dreams. But dates and diamonds aren't
enough to win her heart.
Are those bachelor boys about to become husbands?

Find out in:
To Woo a Wife
Harlequin Presents® #2039, July 1999

To Be a Husband
#2043, August 1999

To Be a Bridegroom
#2051, September 1999

Some men are *meant* to marry!

Available wherever Harlequin books are sold.

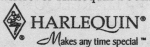 HARLEQUIN®
Makes any time special ™

Look us up on-line at: http://www.romance.net   HPBBROS

HARLEQUIN · CELEBRATES

FIVE DECADES OF ROMANCE

Celebrate!
5 Decades of Romance.
Enjoy Harlequin superstar

DEBBIE MACOMBER

and

RENEE ROSZEL

in

the first of four 2-in-1 Harlequin 50th Anniversary limited collections.

Available in June 1999 at your favorite retail outlet.

HARLEQUIN®

Makes any time special ™

Look us up on-line at: http://www.romance.net   PH50COLL1